Safe with Me

Falling for a Rose Book One

By

Stephanie Nicole Norris

Dedication

To everyone who still believes in love.

Chapter One

Samiyah stared into the light colored mixed drink; her index finger sliding around the rim of the glass in slow rotation. Samiyah thoughts went back to the earlier conversation with her husband.

"Please, Samiyah sign the papers."

She hesitated, *"David if I'm willing to give our marriage another chance shouldn't you be?"*

David sighed, *"I don't want to fight anymore. I love her, and it wouldn't be fair to you if I stayed and pretended we could fix things. Please Samiyah, don't make this harder than it already is. Just sign the papers."*

David slid the papers across the desk and handed Samiyah the very ink pen they'd used to sign the deed on their house, with their mortgage company's name written across it. Her eyes watered, and fresh tears stained her face. She swallowed back a lump in her throat and quickly wipe the tears away.

"Fine," she said through gritted teeth. *Samiyah didn't want to cry in front of him; he didn't deserve any more of her tears. After all, he was the one who cheated. David should be the one crying, but Samiyah couldn't help but feel like she was at a funeral. With a heavy heart,*

Samiyah scribbled her name and tossed the pen and papers at him.

"Now get out!" She needed him gone and fast. Her breakdown was imminent, and there would be no holding back. It was something he couldn't bear witness to. "Get out!" she screamed.

David left without so much as a backward glance. Now she was sitting in Terrance's Sports Bar and Grill nursing her third Mimosa.

"Excuse me," Samiyah lifted her finger to get the bartender's attention.

"Yes ma'am," he tossed a hand towel over his shoulder.

"Please don't call me ma'am, it makes me feel old. My name is Sa-mi-yah. Let me have another Mimosa, please."

The bartender scrutinized her face, taking note of the glazed look in her eyes.

"Are you sure? I can't serve you if you're drunk, and you'd have to sit here another hour before I could let you leave."

A giggle bubbled up from her throat, but her expression remained strained.

"Are you serious?"

He folded his arms and straightened his posture. "It's house rules, ma'am." At the mention of him calling her ma'am, Samiyah rolled her eyes and let out an abysmal breath.

"Samiyah, my name is Sa-mi-yah, and if you don't mind mister..." she waited for him to tell his name. When

2

he didn't she said, "bartender, I'm not drunk, just a little tipsy. And, I don't plan on going away anytime soon, so if you don't mind, how about that drink." The bartender peered at her once more before turning to make her drink. A fresh glass appeared in front of her, he removed the empty glass and produced a napkin.

"Merci," she said.

"Hey beautiful, would you like some company?" The man held his hand out. "I'm Lamar."

Samiyah didn't even bother to look at him. She knew it was the guy from the pool table who'd been giving her a goofy grin the entire night. Instead, she stood, took another sip of her drink emptying the contents, and placed the glass down heavier than she should've, receiving a stern look from the bartender. Her hands rose in surrender, "Won't happen again." She turned to walk off, without offering Lamar acknowledgment.

Lamar reached, snatching her arm. "You're very rude for such a beautiful lady. You know I've paid for your tab tonight, or didn't you notice you weren't being charged?"

Samiyah snatched her arm away from him. "You should get your money back then. I can pay for the drinks myself."

Lamar blocked her exit, grabbing her arm again; this time with a little force. "Listen you undeserving— Aaaah man what the—!" Lamar screamed when a hand landed on his shoulder practically dislocating it.

"Didn't your mother teach you never to put your hands on a lady, or did she dump you on the side of the road before she had a chance to?"

Samiyah's head whipped toward the dark menacing voice, riding the sculpted edges of a handsome specimen. Sure, she'd had enough drinks to blur her vision slightly, but Samiyah refused to believe the image before her was fictitious. A baseball cap rested on his head, but she had a full view of his masculine features; piercing hazel brown eyes, a thick nose, and tempting lips. His broad shoulders sat strong enough to withstand the force of an offensive line. Samiyah didn't notice when the other guy ran off. Her only focus was on the gorgeous brother standing mere inches in front of her.

"Are you okay?" His baritone voice played with her ear drums.

"I am now," she responded.

"I'm Jonas."

"Samiyah Manhattan."

Jonas held out a hand. "It's a shame we have to meet on such hostile terms, Samiyah Manhattan."

She accepted his pro-offered hand, and a jolt of electricity caused her to pull back, surprised and unnerved.

"Interesting," he said.

"I'm sorry, I just..."

"No explanation needed. That guy has been eyeing you all night."

"And how would you know?"

"You're not easy to miss."

Neither are you, she thought.

"Are you here alone?"

"Yes."

"In that case, I'm holding myself personally liable for your well-being, that is, for the remainder of the night."

A tinge of heat rippled through Samiyah, warming her body from head to toe.

"I mean we don't want anyone else getting any ideas."

This time Samiyah grinned. "Now who's explaining?"

"Touché."

The French term didn't go over her head, and Samiyah's interest was officially peaked. Unable to look away, she watched as Jonas' eyes bore into her soul, his delicious lips lifting into a partial smile. What was going on? One minute she was sitting there thinking about her divorce and the next she was flirting with a handsome stranger.

"I don't think I'll be much company."

Jonas stood to her side and opened his arm linking them together.

"I don't believe that for a second," he said, guiding them to his table that sat secluded in the rear of the bar. Within seconds of them taking their seats, a waitress appeared.

"Hi, I'm Sasha, I'll be your server for tonight," she kept her eyes on Jonas. "How can I help you?"

"I would like a strawberry mimosa," Samiyah said, waving her hand in the air to get Sasha's attention."

Reluctantly, the waitress glanced towards her. "Of course." Without missing a beat, Sasha's focus went back to Jonas.

"A glass of water for now," he said.

"Whatever you need, just let me know." The waitress sashayed away.

Samiyah relaxed in her chair and crossed her legs. "You really have them eating out of the palm of your hands, don't you?"

"Them?"

"Isn't it obvious? I might as well be invisible."

Jonas' midnight eyes roamed across her. "Hardly," he said.

"Looks like you've got an admirer," she joked.

"I hadn't noticed."

"Sure you didn't."

Jonas traced the outline of her full lips and imagined how soft they would feel against his. Samiyah's hair sat in a curly bun atop her head; her ears pierced with diamond studs, chestnut brown eyes, and ginger skin.

"Thanks for helping me back there."

Jonas gaze followed her long sleek neck down to her breasts that sat perkily on her chest underneath the thin thigh high summer dress. "Anytime." Samiyah squirmed under his grueling inspection and all of a sudden, she was thirsty. Whatever he was doing to her was causing her body to heat up by the second; making her mouth dry like the Sahara Desert.

Jonas had observed Samiyah sitting at the bar earlier. As soon as her sexy legs carried her through the door with eyes cast down and a pout on her gorgeous face, she'd caught every man's attention in the place. It wasn't until he'd come to her defense that he caught a real glimpse of the natural beauty. She was breathtakingly stunning. Jonas had seen his fair share of attractive women, but Samiyah was the epitome of exquisiteness, exotically so. When she reached to shake his hand the sting he felt rattled him, and Jonas knew she'd felt the same by the way she snatched back her hand.

There was an instant connection with her that was uncanny, and he was still trying to figure it out as he continued to read her. Sasha emerged with their drinks.

"If there is anything else you want, or need let me know, and I'll be happy to get it for you." She spoke once again only referring to Jonas.

"He has everything he needs, trust me," Samiyah snapped. She'd already caught her husband cheating, she wasn't in the mood to deal with a woman flirting right in her face as if she was chop liver, even if Jonas didn't belong to her. Sasha turned and left just as fast as she'd come.

Jonas lips curved lazily. "I have everything that I need," he questioned.

Samiyah felt flushed. Wrapping her hand around the glass, she took a sip out of the straw, taking the alcoholic drink down halfway.

"Maybe you should slow down a little," Jonas injected.

Samiyah pursed her lips, and Jonas' gaze dropped down to them. "Why would I do that?" Her voice was sultry and enchanting now.

"Do you always drink like this?"

She shrugged. "No."

"Then maybe... you should slow down."

"What are you going to do if I don't, spank me?"

His eyebrow arched and Jonas' next words were pronounced slow and methodical. "Your alcohol consumption is impairing your judgment."

"Maybe I want my judgment to be impaired."

Samiyah flirted shamelessly with him without a care in the world. The life as she knew it had just been turned upside down and sitting across from Jonas with the liquid courage pouring through her blood stream, ignited a flame in her that needed to be put out. Jonas drank his water in one gulp and returned the glass to the table. His tongue moistened his lips turning Samiyah's flame into a running torch. She squeezed her thighs together in an attempt to keep her body's libido under control.

"Where are your car keys," he asked.

Samiyah removed the keys and slid them across the table. Jonas caught them before they fell off the edge. Although Jonas was a stranger, Samiyah trusted him, or maybe she'd had too much alcohol after all.

"I'm taking you home. I'll bring you back to get your car tomorrow."

"No," she said plainly.

"I'm not letting you drive home; it's out of the question."

"I meant no, I'm not going home."

"A friends, family members, your," he hesitated, "spouse? Tell me where to take you, and that's where you're going."

"Take me to your home, Jonas."

His name had never sounded so tantalizing. If she hadn't had so many drinks maybe he would have. But he

8

never took a woman to his home. It was nothing for him to grab a hotel room. However, he felt a raw need to keep Samiyah close. He stood and reached for her hand helping her out of the seat. Opening his wallet, he dropped a few twenty-dollar bills on the table and escorted her out of Terrance's Sports Bar and Grill.

Chapter Two

Sun rays crept into the room sending a display of light across Samiyah's face. It was the dawn of a new day, and the intrusion caused her to groan and turn her head away from the patio doors. Slowly, Samiyah's eyes fluttered opened. She had a notion to stay in bed and sleep the day away. The soft, comfortable pillow top mattress was everything she needed for a good night's rest. The smell of bacon lingered in the air. *I could really use something to eat.* But who was cooking, she lived alone? Samiyah clutched the sheets and sat upright in bed.

A dizzy spell fell over her making her temples throb, bringing on an intense headache. Again, she groaned and massaged her head. The bed that held her in a slumber was huge and the room unfamiliar. Underneath the sheets Samiyah's legs were bare and the oversized jersey she wore smelled of a cologne she couldn't recognize. Quickly, Samiyah left the bed and shuffled to the open bathroom door but halted in her tracks when she noticed what looked like huge belts decorating a shelf. Curiosity getting the better of her, Samiyah strode over to the shelf to gain a closer look. The green strap was made of Ferrari leather with a gold plaque in the middle.

The words written on the plaque said, World Champion, with the flag from each country embedded on the trim. There were gold coins on the belt with a picture inside. Samiyah's face lit up and the memories from last night came back to her. It was Jonas' face; the supremely handsome gentleman that saved her from the creep at the bar. Her eyes traveled to the belts sitting next to each other, and she felt a small sense of pride. Samiyah didn't even know Jonas, but these trophies were beautiful.

"I don't fight anymore; I retired five years ago."

Samiyah whipped around and staggered. "I'm sorry, I didn't mean to pry."

He folded his arms. "It's not a problem."

Samiyah surveyed Jonas; he was just as handsome now as he was in her drunken haze, even more so. His caramel skin was toned showing muscular arms and a chiseled bare chest. Samiyah reached up and touched her mouth to make sure her tongue wasn't hanging out. When she found it wasn't, she quickly slid her hand back down. Jonas seemed amused. Samiyah blinked several times trying to clear her thoughts. "Um, I guess I'm in your house?" The question was rhetorical.

"You are," he confirmed. "Don't worry, you're safe with me."

Samiyah didn't doubt it even though she probably should. "I'm not in the habit of going home with strangers you know."

"That's good to know."

"Did we have sex last night?"

There it was that award-winning smile she knew lingered behind those hinted grins he gave out last night.

"You don't remember?" He teased.

Samiyah gasped, throwing her hands to her mouth. Jonas stepped closer invading her space. He pinched her chin. "I assure you, if we made love, I would never let you forget it."

He winked and Samiyah was sure her panties were in need of changing. Wasn't it enough that he was standing there bare-chested looking like Hercules? With just the slightest touch he'd sent shivers down her spine.

"You undressed me," she stated.

"I did," and it was the hardest thing he'd ever done. By the time they'd made it to his penthouse, Samiyah was asleep. Jonas wanted to wake her, but he could tell she needed the rest. So instead, he carried her to his private elevator, keyed in a code on the security pad, and rode to the top with her in his arms. She smelled of vanilla and coffee beans which were ironic since she'd been drinking mimosas all night. Her skin was a smooth ginger, and her hair was thin with a natural wave texture. He wanted to take that clip out and see her tresses fall. Inside, Jonas carried her to the bedroom, laid her on the king size bed and released her mane. It tumbled down stopping right below her breasts. "Beautiful," he'd whispered. Undressing her was torture. Whenever his hands grazed her skin, he felt a heated tinge that refused to go away.

Her body was perfect. A black lace bra adorned her perky breasts, and the lace panties were snug around her curvaceous hips. Jonas hastily covered her in his jersey. Seeing Samiyah in her bare minimum teased his libido. Jonas had taken a cold shower to work off the tension that seeped into his bones. Now standing in front of her he yearned to do what he didn't get a chance to do the night before. With a disregard for repercussions, Jonas reached for her face his hand hovering just below her chin. Just short of touching her, Jonas could feel the ball of energy that clung between them.

"Do you feel that," he asked.

Samiyah closed her eyes, her chest rising and falling. Of course, she felt it. In a breathless response she said, "Yes."

Jonas dipped his head bringing his lips to hers. A flare of warmth buzzed through them. His hands slid into her wavy mane and the other around her waist pulling her firmly against a solidly built chest. Samiyah's arms casually slipped around his neck as their mouths engaged. There was an intense tingling in her spine that was making its way down to her vagina. Their moans mixed and mingled; bouncing off their tongues in a vivacious musical. It was Jonas who paused first. Samiyah groaned, she didn't want to think, she just wanted to do.

"What's wrong," she asked.

His heavy lids were aimed at her lips. "We're about to reach the point of no return, Miss Manhattan."

He waited for her acceptance, but at the mention of her ex-husband's last name Samiyah recoiled and pulled away from him. Jonas silently rebuked himself. Samiyah ran her fingers through her hair in frustration.

"I've gotta go." She side-stepped him. "Where are my clothes?"

Jonas nodded to the closet, and with haste Samiyah grabbed the items, running past him to the bathroom. He stepped to the door to slow her down, but she shut it in his face. He raised his hand to knock but thought better of it. *Was it something I said?* He wondered. On the other side, Samiyah leaned her back into the door and slid down until her butt hit the cold marble tile. Her head fell forward to her knees, and she covered herself with her arms.

What was she doing? And what was this weird chemistry about? Samiyah was done with men, right? She had made up her mind to enjoy the single life and take her career to the next level. That was after she'd finished mourning the death of her marriage. But in the middle of her crisis, in walks this robust, enticing, scorching, creation that was leaving her breathless and vulnerable.

The ambiance she felt when around Jonas was unnatural and plain sorcery. Even now, sitting on the opposite side of the door, her body yearned to be with him. Her head snapped up, that was it. She thought. Sex. She needed it, craved it and he was a perfect candidate. She'd played by the rules, been the doting housewife, honored her vows, and what did she get in return? Samiyah rose from the floor and removed the jersey in one smooth motion. The reflection in the full mirror revealed a sexy siren in a black sheer lace panties and bra. Her hair was tousled like a lioness. Samiyah ran the faucet and splashed warm water over her face. She took the tube of toothpaste, squirted some on her finger and massaged her gums and teeth. She grabbed the mouthwash and gargled, then washed her mouth out with water. While the courage was still potent, Samiyah dried her hands and left the bathroom in search of Jonas. She found him in the kitchen with a glass of orange juice raised to his lips. When he saw her, he dropped the glass on the counter and waited for her to approach him. She did, slow and seductive. Standing in front of him, she spoke.

"I was wondering," the mint mouthwash tingled her lips, "If you were hungry."

Jonas reached for her, wrapping his arms around her waist, lifting her with ease onto the wide marble counter. He cocked his head to the side and kissed her chin, face, and neck; biting her shoulder before moving down to her breasts. Keeping her on edge, Jonas leaned into Samiyah, allowing her to feel what she was doing to him.

With her head back, Samiyah moaned as Jonas moved to her navel, laying kisses all over her stomach. A phone rang, but it sounded like it was on another planet. Jonas' hands caressed every inch of her body down to her toes. He kissed her inner thighs and blew lightly over her sex. Samiyah panted and her body torched with every touch from him. Jonas reached out and hit a button on the front of the refrigerator that dropped ice cubes in his hand. He put a frozen cube in his mouth and rubbed it against the core of her sheer panties. Samiyah called out to God as a mingle of heat and coldness from his resplendent mouth flooded her, sending her into sexual overdrive.

The phone rang again, and this time the ringtone was familiar. As bad as Samiyah wanted to ignore it, she couldn't. Samiyah grabbed his face and pulled Jonas towards her watching him swallow the ice and lick his lips. She shuttered; quickly regretting why she'd made him stop. His eyes sat low, and the growth on his face tingled her fingers.

"I'm sorry," Samiyah panted lightly, "that's my office calling. I'll be right back."

She wiggled to hop down, and he blocked her path. "This isn't over," he promised sinking his lips into hers. Samiyah shut her eyes and salivated at the taste of his tongue. Her phone started up again, and Jonas reluctantly released her. Halfheartedly, Samiyah went and answered it. Jonas knew what was coming next, another cold shower.

Chapter Three

Jonas removed his suit jacket and placed it on his high back office chair. There was a knock at the door and Stacy, his secretary, leaned in the doorway.

"Well, you're fashionably late. Would you like coffee?"

"Yes, thank you."

"The board meeting starts in ten minutes." She left the room and returned shortly with his coffee. "Just the way you like it," she purred. He glanced at her.

"I'll be there in two minutes."

Jonas was the Chairman and CEO of Rose Bank and Trust Credit Union, which had over thirty branches across the southwest and southeast region. He'd taken over the company six years ago when his dad, Christopher Lee Rose, purchased another thriving corporation, and business was better than ever. Jonas was looking to expand the branches to the northeast and west regions which kept him in daily business meetings. Jonas took a sip of his coffee and powered his MAC. It motorized within seconds, and his thoughts traveled to Samiyah. There was an emergency at her job leaving only enough time to stop by her home and change her clothes. Jonas had dropped her off in front of an office building with a promise to pick her up for lunch so she could retrieve her vehicle from Terrance's.

An image of Samiyah's delectable mouth stood out in his mind. Jonas knew when he first laid eyes on her lips, that they would be soft and edible. It was no doubt the two had sexual chemistry, but he couldn't shake the feeling that there was more between them. Jonas chuckled, that was just nonsense. They would have mind blowing sex and maybe call each other here and there, but there would be nothing more. Jonas didn't have time for that nor did he want it. He had too much going on, and the only women that clung to him did so because of his stature and heavy bank account.

But she didn't even know who you were.

He dismissed those thoughts immediately. Women could be very manipulative. There was another knock at his door.

"They're ready," Stacy said.

"You know, Stacy, you can always pick up the phone and dial my extension; there's no need for you to come to my door to deliver all the news that comes across your desk." He entwined his fingers resting his forearm on the desk.

"I don't mind at all, Mr. Rose, anything for you."

A flirtatious smile crossed her face. She lingered a moment longer before making her way back to her desk. He shook his head. *Prime example*, he thought. When he stood to leave the office, his cell phone rang. Grabbing the Iphone, he noted the unfamiliar number.

With a stern voice, Jonas answered, "Rose."

"Hey, hey, hey, long time no hear. You got rich on me and disappeared. I've missed you man, what have you been up to?"

Jonas squinted. "Who is this?"

The caller guffawed. "Now I know it's been a long time since we spoke but surely my voice isn't unrecognizable."

Jonas turned his back to the door. "Kevin?" he whispered.

"So you do remember me after all. Whew, you pulled a fast one on me there!"

"How did you get this number," Jonas asked all but annoyed.

"Oh come on now, is that any way to treat an old friend? You know I have my ways. I can get just about whatever. If you need anything, let me know, and I can get it for you. We may be able to help each other out."

"I doubt it."

Jonas was uninterested and busy, and his flat tone said as much.

"Man you're cold! What happened to the man I knew that was down for whatever?"

"That man is dead; he was dumb and young."

"I know he's still around somewhere. Check this out, I know you're retired and all but I have a couple of guys who are undefeated and have put fifty million dollars on the line that they can beat you. Now, I know they'd be digging their own graves, but you know what they say, you can lead a horse to water, but you can't make him drink. Right?"

"I'm not fighting."

"Just hear me out, it's one night. If you beat one, it's fifty million dollars. If you beat all three, it's one hundred and fifty million. You can't pass this up it's a load of money involved."

"I just did."

Jonas ended the called and put his phone on silent, leaving his office for the conference room.

"I would say good morning, but good afternoon would be more appropriate. Are you doing okay?"

"Actually I'm feeling much better."

Claudia Stevens, Samiyah's business partner and best friend, closed the office door and made herself comfortable in one of the leather chairs that sat in front of Samiyah's desk. They owned a small business in the Chicago area and specialized in financial planning.

"You know you can tell me anything, right?"

"Yes, I'm not holding back. I'm fine."

Claudia didn't believe her; she studied Samiyah. "Okay, what's going on?"

Samiyah wondered if she should tell her about Jonas, then opted for another conversation first. She told her about the conversation with her now ex-husband David. Rehashing the details brought tears to her eyes. Samiyah and David had been going through a divorce for over a year. They'd decided to settle out of court, but at the last minute Samiyah wanted to fight for her marriage. She didn't know why. She wasn't even in love anymore, but she felt a sense of duty to make sure she'd done everything she could to make it work. In the end, it was David who wanted to leave.

"Honey, I absolutely don't know why you're here. I told you to take some time off," Claudia said. "We have Selena and Octavia here to fill in. It's not a problem, I've told you this."

"That was my plan. I could use a little time, but what about the emergency phone call I got this morning? Selena didn't sound so sure of herself. I had to calm her down and tell her to serve the clients coffee and croissants until I got here. She should know that much."

Claudia waved her off. "Girl, Selena had a client in her office and three in the waiting room, and she was the only one here. Since she has no idea what's going on in your personal life, she wasn't aware you would be taking time off. I was running a little late but trust me I got this."

Samiyah pursed her lips. "I don't know. What had you running late this morning?"

"Let's just say I had a long night."

Samiyah shook her head and laughed, "What did I tell you about picking up random guys at the club? You've got to be over it by now."

Samiyah was one to talk; didn't she just get through seducing a stranger this morning? Had she not woken up in his bed? Samiyah threw those thoughts to the back of her mind.

"Yeah, yeah, I hear you, but you're not the only one who wants a love life."

"You can have it; I'm done with it."

"What does that mean? You're not crossing over to the other side are you?"

Samiyah threw her head back and laughed, "That's not what I meant."

"Well let's just be clear." They both laughed. "It's good to see you smile, you've been so down lately," Claudia mentioned.

"It feels good to laugh. Let's have a quick pow-wow to make sure Selena and Octavia are on top of their game. I can't very well leave if they're feeling under pressure."

Claudia picked up the phone and dialed each of their extensions. "Come see us, please," she said when they answered.

Selena Strauss glided into the room with a notepad in hand. She was fresh out of college and always willing to learn. During the interview process, Samiyah took an immediate liking to her, offering her a career pending a clear criminal background check. Octavia Davenport was close behind her. Octavia had six years of experience in financial planning before coming on board, but she was used to having her boss breathing down her neck.

Things worked differently at S & M Financial Advisors. "Do either of you have clients right now?" Samiyah asked.

Selena spoke first, "I've got one coming in fifteen minutes."

"My next appointment will be here any moment," Octavia glanced at her watch.

"This will be quick, have a seat."

They obliged. "Selena, I know being here is new for you and Octavia I know you're also getting used to the way things work around here. Do either of you have any concerns or questions?"

"This is about this morning, isn't it?" Selena inquired.

"Yes and no," Samiyah confirmed. "Claudia and I want to make sure you ladies are both comfortable with your workload. When everyone is comfortable with what they're doing, things will work smoothly, and that's what we all want."

"I wasn't sure if I needed to reschedule some of your appointments that came in this morning. When you didn't show up, I kind of freaked out. Sorry," Selena said biting her lip.

"That's my fault," Claudia spoke up. "Samiyah will be taking some time off for the next week, and during that period I'll be handling her clients."

"That's when she can make it to work on time." Samiyah leveled her with a glare. Selena and Octavia chuckled and cut their eyes at Claudia.

"Okay, Okay," she repeated, "You got me, I won't be late anymore."

"Ladies I want you to know if you're not sure about something, don't panic. Call my cell, tell me what's going on and I'll walk you through it." Samiyah glanced at the wall clock. "You should go check to see if your clients are in. Oh, and relax, we are not going to be breathing down your neck. We trust you'll get your jobs done right, that's why we hired you. There are always breakfast croissants in the kitchen. Our longtime friend Larry comes in to bring fresh sandwiches every morning. He delivers to everyone in this office building. Help yourselves."

"Thank you." Octavia and Selena smiled.

"Oh have you ladies picked out your dresses for the auction?"

Selena clasped her hands together, "Yes, I'm so excited."

"I've got mine too; we went at the same time," Octavia said.

"Oh, nice! I'd love to see them," Samiyah said.

"I'll show you a picture in a minute," Octavia stuck her head out the door, "We've got company ladies."

They left to tend to their clients.

"What time are you departing?" Claudia asked.

Samiyah glanced at her wall clock, "In about an hour."

"Oh yeah, I didn't see your car outside, what's wrong with it now?"

A pleasant smile fluttered across Samiyah's face. "About that... after everything that happened with David, I went to a bar for drinks."

"Without me?"

"Oh girl, you were too busy getting your groove back."

"I could've found my groove wherever you were. Don't try and put this on me!"

"Did you hear what you just said? That's an indication that you need to stop picking up randoms!"

"Don't change the subject," Claudia said dismissing her last statement.

Samiyah gave details about the bar incident and waking up in Jonas' bed. She left out the part about her seduction. This time Claudia threw her head back and yelled, "Oooou! Oooou! Oooou!"

"Sssssssh, girl we have clients in the building, have you lost your mind!"

Claudia cupped a hand over her mouth, "I'm sorry I'm just so excited for you. He is just what you need."

"How do you know that? I don't even know him, Claudia. He was just mister right now, that's it! So don't get all extra because I know how you are."

"Listen, you can't lie to me. A handsome man comes to your rescue; then you slept in his bed, and he didn't take advantage? Are you crazy?" Claudia threw her arms up. "I can't ever catch a break like that. You lucky girl, I'm so jealous."

Samiyah cracked a smile and shook her head, "You are a piece of work, you know that?"

"I do, but you know I'm right. You better not let that man slip through your fingers!"

"Claudia please, I've been divorced one day. Does it look like I'm trying to throw myself into another relationship? And another thing, what makes you think this man wants one? He's some famous ex-boxer anyway. I'm sure he has plenty of women to go around."

"Famous ex-boxer? What's his full name?"

Samiyah shrugged her shoulders, "Jonas Alexander Rose."

Claudia's eyes almost popped out of their sockets. "As in one of the seven of the Rose brother's clan?"

Samiyah thought about it for a minute. She'd heard about the famous Rose brothers and some of their ventures, but she'd never given it much thought. She shrugged.

"Possibly."

Claudia got up out of her seat and left Samiyah's office. When she returned, Claudia slapped a magazine down on Samiyah's desk and pointed, "Is Jonas Alexander Rose this brother right here?"

The Time magazine read;

The 100 Most Influential People in The World, Jonas Alexander Rose, One of Chicago's Elite Seven of the Rose Brothers.

Seven insanely gorgeous men graced the cover, with Jonas standing in the forefront. They were all impeccably dressed in tailored suits, with Jonas wearing boxing gloves. His pose showed strength and power with his boxing gloves meeting up fist to fist in the middle of his stance. His intimidating glare was transparent in his posture, causing a tingle to run down Samiyah's spine.

"Girl your mouth is hanging open!" Claudia said. "I take it by your silence this is him."

Samiyah's office phone rang. With Samiyah still speechless, Claudia reached down and hit the speaker button. "Samiyah Manhattan," Claudia announced.

"It's Selena, Mrs. Manhattan; you have a visitor."

Samiyah and Claudia turned towards the glass office windows simultaneously. Jonas Alexander Rose stood in the waiting room, talking to one of the female clients. Claudia turned back to Samiyah and swatted her across the arm. "You lucky, lucky girl!"

Chapter Four

Jonas opened the passenger door to his 2016 Aston Martin, stepping to the side to allow Samiyah entrance. The blood red exterior was so clean it sparkled in the sunlight. As Samiyah walked up, she caught a glimpse of herself in the luxury sports car's reflection.

"What happened to the car you dropped me off in earlier?" she asked.

"It's being serviced. I have it on a bi-weekly schedule."

Intrigued, Samiyah slid into her seat. Jonas closed the door and strode around to the driver side. The interior of the sport's car was just as stylish and supremely refined.

"How long is your lunch?"

"I'm taking the rest of the day off," Samiyah said.

"In that case, do you have time to enjoy a meal with me?"

Samiyah wondered how this man made everything sound so sexual. Or maybe it was her. Either way, she couldn't seem to turn him down.

"I do," she said.

A grin frolicked around his lips, "Fasten your seatbelt."

Samiyah did as she was told. At the start of the ignition, the car hummed and Bryson Tillers hit song *Don't* began to play. Jonas pulled off, making a left on Singapore. The luxury sports car merged onto the highway with ease as Bryson's soft melody serenaded them.

Jonas' eyes left the road long enough to notice Samiyah sitting tensely with one hand gripping the door handle and the other in a tight fist in her lap.

"Are you okay," he asked.

"I've never gone this fast in a car before. Could you please slow down."

Her voice was ambivalent yet anxious. Jonas reached over and grabbed her hand interlacing their fingers. "Do you trust me," he asked.

Samiyah wavered, "Yes."

"Are you sure?" he tightened his grip.

The warmth from his hand tingled her palm sending a buzz crawling up her arm that enveloped her. There was a throb between her thighs and her heart raced.

"Didn't I tell you, you're safe with me? I wouldn't put you in harm's way; you should know that by now."

Jonas spoke while watching the road. When his hazel eyes looked back at Samiyah, she bit down on her lip.

"Relax, I've got you."

He turned back to the road and switched lanes driving around two cars. The Aston Martin moved with the grace of a panther and the speed of a cheetah. Samiyah didn't know how much more of this sexual interaction she could take. They were interrupted earlier, but she was ready to finish what they started.

"Pull over," she said.

"Okay, I'll slow down, we're almost there."

Jonas exited the freeway and made a right onto one financial place. "Is that better?" He glanced at her.

Samiyah was coming out of her clothes. "I don't think you understand; I said pull over."

She was feeling downright naughty and wild, but she would blame that on the speed of the sports car. Jonas' gaze faltered, and he whipped the luxury car into the parking garage into the first spot he could find.

"Do you have a condom?" she asked. Jonas hit a button on the glove compartment, it dropped open, and he reached in and grabbed a magnum. Samiyah pulled her panties off but left her bra clasped. She reached for his pants, and he grabbed her wrists.

"Slow down..."

Jonas pulled Samiyah into his lap and let the seat all the way back. She moved her hips in circles grinding against him. There was evidence of his arousal almost instantly. Jonas dug his hands into her hips, lifting her with ease, mounting her on his face. Her thighs hung on the side of his head making Samiyah completely vulnerable to his magnificent mouth; when his lips moved Samiyah gasped and let out a sharp cry. Her vanilla fragrance drowned him, and his heart thundered. Jonas' nostrils flared at the uninhibited hunger attacking his senses. He turned his head slightly and bit the inside of her thigh like a beast about to pull his prey off for slaughter. The heat from his mouth mixed with the animalistic mark sent a shrill down Samiyah's back. Her head fell, and her mouth parted on a fleeting moan. Jonas covered her peach with his entire mouth sucking on her lips. With his tongue he invaded the wettest part of her, massaging her softness. He played around her clitoris determined to drive her insane. His lips closed around her as he sucked, sending a vibration with his tongue that rendered her useless.

Samiyah twitched and turned, rotating her hips. "Sssss...aaaah...Jonas..." she moaned. His name became music to his ears, and Jonas fiddled her lips as if her folds were a playing instrument. Samiyah tried to move, but Jonas grabbed her ample bottom holding her in place.

A vibration trembled from her body, informing Jonas that she was close to her release.

"Oh my God, Jonas, Jonas, Jonas..."

Samiyah continued to call out his name and beg for mercy. He reached behind her and unclasped her bra and it fell loose.

"Jonas..." she called breathlessly trying to warn him of her impending eruption.

His long solid arms crept up her spine circling to her breasts. He fondled her areolas with his fingers and lapped on her clitoris like only she could provide the water that would quench his thirst. There was no more pleading with Samiyah now. All she could do was moan and scream; her body jerking going into convulsions as she rode his face. Samiyah quivered uncontrollably and felt out of her mind.

"I can't...I can't..." she repeated trying her best to get away from him, but Jonas was punishing her. A beautiful punishment no doubt. Samiyah wanted this, and he sucked and licked on her until there was nothing left. "What are you trying to do to me," she cried. He lifted her and eased her back down to his lap.

"Ruining you for all others," he responded.

Samiyah smirked and reached for the condom that sat in the passenger seat but was interrupted by a knock on the window.

"Excuse me," the valet attended said. "You have to have a ticket to park. He tried peeking through the tinted window of the Aston Martin. Samiyah scrambled to the back seat while Jonas re-adjusted his and cracked the window.

"We're on our way out."

"Thank you, sir." The man walked away.

"Maybe we should resume this later," Jonas said. "Let me feed you."

There it was again, his words making her heart race once more. As Samiyah adjusted her bra and put her clothes back on, she wondered why this man stirred her soul so much. What was it about him that made it easy for Samiyah to say yes? She'd been married to David for six years and not once felt the passion and craving for his love that Jonas pulled out of her.

He got out of the car, and she adjusted her heels checking her reflection in the rearview mirror briefly.

Jonas opened her door and held out his hand. She accepted it, and they walked to the valet station. He offered the key to the valet attendant and received a ticket.

"I'll guide you to the elevators," the valet said.

"There's no need, I've been here before," Jonas responded.

"Enjoy your lunch."

Upon entering the elevators, Jonas checked his Rolex then his phone. Samiyah wondered if he had a wife and kids at home. It wouldn't surprise her; men these days were reckless.

"Waiting on a phone call," she asked.

"As a matter of fact, I am."

"I'm sure she'll call any minute."

Jonas gave her a side eye, "Why Miss Manhattan, is that a hint of jealousy I hear?"

Samiyah guffawed, "Please, why would I be jealous. You would never belong to me."

"And why is that?"

"You're not the type."

Jonas took a second before responding. "Since you know everything, tell me, what type am I, Samiyah?"

The pronunciation of her name sounded like butter melting off his hot tongue. *Focus Samiyah,* she silently scolded herself.

"The type that goes from woman to woman leaving a trail of broken hearts. You're a celebrity, apparently wealthy, attractive, and flirtatious. It's your lifestyle, and I'm fine with it. Has nothing to do with me. Actually, I barely know you. I must be out of my mind with everything I've done with you within the last twenty-four hours; I must be really losing it." She continued to ramble, and Jonas appeared amused.

The elevator doors opened, and they entered the lobby, they walked to another set of elevators that took them up the high rise to Everest Restaurant. The host found the reservation Jonas prematurely made in the hopes that he could get her there, and they were escorted to their dining table. After ordering, Jonas rechecked his Iphone again.

"Why don't you just call her? If you need me to, I'll excuse myself to the bathroom."

He leveled his eyes on her for a long moment. "I'm waiting for the call that my Bentley is ready. It doesn't usually take this long to be serviced unless there's a problem."

"Oh," was all she said.

He smirked, "You say you barely know me, but it seems you've done some homework. This morning you didn't act as if you knew who I was."

"I didn't," Samiyah confirmed. "I saw a magazine with you and six other men on the front. She left out the fact that they were drop dead gorgeous. "I didn't get to read it, but that's when I realized you were thee, Jonas Alexander Rose."

"And you didn't know that when you saw my belts?"

"I didn't connect the dots, remember I met you last night when I had too much to drink."

"Right..." he said.

"By the way, I'm a financial advisor; I'd love to help you with any future planning. Vacations, retirement, marriage, divorce, alimony. I'll even throw in a free consultation."

Jonas folded his hands. "Thank you for your services. I may take you up on your offer, although I'm not married, I don't have any prospects, and when I am married, divorce and alimony will not be an option. I don't make decisions like that lightly. When I take my vows, they will be honored, and only a significant woman will share those vows. And for the record, I don't leave a trail of broken hearts because I'm straightforward. I don't play games. If you're a date, you're a date, if you're a fling, you're a fling, and if you're my wife, then you're the love of my life."

He never took his eyes off of her. His message was well received. Samiyah shifted in her seat under his intense gaze. The server appeared with their food, and they ate. Samiyah's phone rang. Taking a look at the screen, she saw the one number she loathed to see. She glanced at Jonas.

"Don't mind me, please take your call."

She answered, "Yes?"

"Samiyah, I'm trying to get into the house and grab the rest of my belongings, but my key isn't working."

Samiyah was annoyed. "That's because I changed the locks as soon as you left."

David sighed, "Can we not do this song and dance please? I need to get in."

Much to her displeasure she knew he needed to get in. "I'll be there in an hour." She hung up.

Chapter Five

The Aston Martin pulled to a stop in front of Samiyah's townhome.

"Thank you, Jonas; I'll catch a taxi to the bar to pick up my car. She touched his arm, "Lunch was wonderful."

"Indeed, it was. Listen, I don't mind taking you to get your car. It's not a problem at all."

"I couldn't take up any more of your time, but thanks anyway."

"Hey," Jonas spoke. Samiyah turned back to him. "Is everything okay?" He noticed how her mood changed after her phone call.

"My ex-husband is a pain, but I have to take care of this, so it's cool."

Jonas reared his head back to get a look at her house. David was leaning into the front of the townhome trying to get in through a window.

"I'll walk you to your door."

"No please, I don't want to involve you in my messy life. I can handle it. I promise. It's okay."

Samiyah opened the door and quickly made her exit. Jonas watched her. When she stepped to the door an argument instantly ensued. Jonas couldn't shake the overprotectiveness he felt for her. True, he wouldn't let any man be rude to a woman in his presence. However, the need to keep her safe was feeling etched in his soul. When she'd touched him, her soft fingers danced along his skin sending a wave of heat prancing along his nerves. Her touch was dangerous, erotic and downright carnal. However, this was her life, and he didn't owe her anything, and yet...

With his eyes still watching them, David stepped closer getting in Samiyah's face. She folded her arms, defiant with whatever was happening. David screamed something unintelligible and banged his palm against the front door. Swiftly, Jonas exited the Aston Martin. His length and pace taking him to the door within seconds.

"Samiyah, is there a problem?"

She unfolded her arms and spun around caught off guard by his manifestation.

"Man, who are you? Wait you look familiar..." David said rubbing his chin in thought.

Jonas ignored him, keeping his eyes only on Samiyah. "Sweetheart, are you okay?"

Samiyah melted at his endearment when she knew she shouldn't have.

David frowned. "Sweetheart?" he turned to Samiyah, "Man who is this? You know what? Nevermind. I've been gone all of what twenty-four hours and you're already entertaining someone else? Just goes to show that you weren't faithful like you said." He twisted his lips, "I knew it. It's okay though because this pretty boy will only be around long enough to screw you and be off to the next jungle bunny. David laughed, "I thought you were better than that? when he drops you like a bad habit don't say I didn't tell you."

Samiyah turned back to him and released all the pent-up anger she'd been holding back. She slapped him across his face so hard it stung her palm. Holding her finger out at David, Samiyah spoke.

"First, you've been gone for two years now. I just didn't find out about it until a year ago and what I do in this day and time is none of your concern. I could care less how you feel about it. I've felt more passion from this man in twenty-four hours then I felt with you for six years. So why don't you crawl back to your homewrecker! If you want your stuff, it will be on the side of the road in fifteen minutes. You're more than welcome to wait by the trash can while I dump it out!" Rage vibrated through her causing her hands to shake.

David lifted his hand to return her assault, but it was caught in midair by Jonas. "You heard the lady," he said; his voice low and ominous.

David snatched his hand out of Jonas' and swung at him. Big mistake. With ease, Jonas stepped to the side and punched David in the nose causing blood to spring forth.

"Aaaaa!" David wailed covering his face with his hands. "This is not over. I'll sue you!"

"Unhuh, send the bill to my lawyer," Jonas replied.

David scrambled, stretching the length of the yard to his car and jumping in.

"I'm sorry about that," Samiyah said.

She took her keys out and searched for the correct one. Her hand shook as she tried to insert the key. Samiyah was a ball of nerves now. She didn't want to fight anymore; she didn't want to hurt anymore, she just wanted to be left alone. Seeing her struggle, Jonas covered Samiyah's hands with his and removed the keys.

"Is this the right one," he asked.

Samiyah nodded. He opened the door, and they went in. Samiyah flew up the stairs as tears fell from her face. She went into David's closet and grabbed the remaining clothes that hung there and slung them on the bed. Back and forth, back and forth she went about the business of getting his items out. Quickly, she moved to the tall mahogany dresser and removed more items. Her single tears turned into a full outcry, and she dropped to her knees in front of her bed stuffing her face into the sheets.

Warm, strong arms enveloped her, lifting her up from the floor cradling her in his chest. Samiyah cried and spoke, "I don't know what I did wrong? Why was I not good enough? I did everything for him and then some. And all he did was crush me!"

Jonas lifted Samiyah's chin. "He's a clown. Don't ever feel like you weren't enough. A real man knows when he's in the presence of a jewel and the right man will love you unconditionally with no strings attached."

They shared a riveted stimulating moment. Jonas kissed away Samiyah's tears, his lips landing on each spot that was stained by her sadness. Jonas was sincere about his words. Although he hadn't known her but a minute, Jonas knew she was intelligent, driven, and determined, and he wanted to know all there was to know about her. That surprised him. Jonas kissed her lips and dried her eyes. He wanted to teach David a lesson, but he was aware that fighting him would be unfair. David wouldn't have a chance. It was that moment when he knew he'd do anything to protect her. It was quite silly actually, but Jonas couldn't reason with the emotions that built up every time she talked or laughed, nor could he explain them. He hated to see her cry. It pained him to the point of lunacy. Samiyah drew away from Jonas, and stood to her feet. A regretful sigh escaped her.

"Jonas, I need you to leave."

Taken out of his reverie, Jonas cast a long look at her. "Did I do something wrong?" He thought about what occurred outside and wondered if she was upset about him for getting involved.

"I just need to be alone right now to clear my thoughts." She cast her eyes downward and ran a hand through her hair. "Don't worry about my car; I'll get a taxi to pick it up."

"I don't want you to take a taxi, it's unnecessary."

"I suppose it's a good thing it's not up to you then," she snapped.

His brows furrowed and he slid his hands into his pockets. Jonas wanted to question her further but instead, he tilted his head in agreement.

"Whatever you wish."

With that, he turned and descended the stairs. When Samiyah heard the door shut she sank to the carpet. It was true, she needed to get a grip on reality. She'd just spent the last six years of her life in a marriage that ultimately failed. The last thing she wanted to do was spend more of her life with a man who would be here today and gone tomorrow. She thought about David's words.

'This pretty boy will only be around long enough to screw you and be off to the next jungle bunny.'

The truth was it shouldn't have mattered to her, but it did. As much as Samiyah tried to convince herself that she was done with men, she wanted someone to love her as completely as she love them in return. As it was now, Samiyah was damaged, and who could ever love her like that?

A gust of wind spun past Jonas' face as his feet hit the pavement in a sprint. It was unusually hot and humid early this Monday morning which meant he could look forward to another scorching afternoon. Jonas' long strides carried him down the riverbank and through a courtyard surrounded by blooming garden flowers and trees. Determined to beat his brother's record of one mile in nine minutes, Jonas increased his speed. The challenge had been well accepted since he could use it to focus on anything other than her.

It had been a week since Jonas left Samiyah's townhouse, puzzled about her abrupt withdrawal from him. Many times, Jonas told himself to let it go, but thoughts of Samiyah controlled him. A part of him detested it. No woman had ever come close to filling his mind with saccharine images, and he was still trying to figure out what it was about Samiyah that made him want to find out.

"Time!" Jaden yelled bringing the run to an end. "Brother, you've gotten worse!" Jaden threw his head back and howled with laughter.

Jonas gritted his teeth and snatched the stopwatch out of Jaden's hands bewildered at the time displayed. Fifteen minutes thirty seconds. With a ravenous whip of his head toward his brother, Jonas grabbed Jaden's shirt.

"You played me!" He seethed.

Jaden snatched his arm flinging it away from him. "You played yourself!"

Jonas suppressed a growl and strolled to a nearby bench to sit down. He bent slightly, resting his forearm on his thighs. Jaden joined him.

"What's going on with you? Last week you hit eleven minutes. Talk to me."

Jonas slid him a glance then sat against the bench allowing his head to fall back, the sun shining on his face. He knew his brother would tease him about what he had to say, but it was imperative that he get it out.

"I met a woman," Jonas started. "I can't seem to get her off my mind."

To say Jaden was more than intrigued was an understatement. He knew his brother's history with women, and they were never given a second thought.

"Continue," Jaden said.

Jonas relived the activities between him and Samiyah, all the way up to the point of his eviction.

"But you've had beautiful women before, so what's so different about her?" Jaden questioned.

"You don't understand," Jonas began. "The atmosphere when I'm around her is compelling. She's sexy, daring, charming, intelligent, but most importantly, I want to listen to her when she speaks. I feel the need to solve her problems. I feel like she's my responsibility. How do you explain that?"

Jaden gave his brother a slap on the back, "Sounds like wife material to me."

A crease formed at the edge of Jonas' eyes following through to his forehead. "Nah, now you're tripping."

Jaden held his hands up. "No you're trippin. If I even come close to finding a woman that makes emotions rise in me like that. I'm taking her off the market, fast."

"Let's go; I need to get back to the office."

"You always change the subject when you get uncomfortable with the topic. What are you going to do," Jaden asked.

"Don't you know, after all that, I didn't even get her number," Jonas replied, shaking his head.

"But you know where she works, right?"

He did, and he knew where his brother was going with this.

"I'm not here to push you off the deep end, but if you ever want to find out if this thing you feel has merit, you know what you need to do," Jaden offered.

Jonas didn't respond. Instead, he rose from the bench, and they jogged their way back to his car.

Chapter Six

A round of applause reverberated throughout the conference room. Standing confident and self-assured, Jonas commanded everyone's attention. Rose Bank and Trust Credit Union had just expanded to the north, with its first branch located in the heart of New York City.

"In celebration of all your hard work and efforts, I'm taking you all on vacation to San Juan, Puerto Rico."

Another wave of applause along with cheers and whistles chorused as the board members rejoiced over the news.

"Even though we'll be on vacation, some of our biggest sponsors will also be attending with us. It's only fair that everyone who had a hand in this venture enjoy the festivities."

"Even the modeling agency? Their donation was helpful to the success of this expansion." A man in the back of the room insisted.

A couple of snickers were heard, and another guy agreed. A pleasant smile covered Jonas' face. "Yes, Connor and Mike," he said making a point to call them both out. "A Taste of Elegance Modeling Agency is invited."

The men whooped while some of the women rolled their eyes and shook their heads.

"Settle down boys. I expect you'll be on your best behavior," Jonas winked.

The men hooted, "Yes sir, we will."

"This is a four-day-three-night vacation so get your affairs in order and dress accordingly. There is champagne in the break room for anyone who would like a glass. No seconds, drink responsibly."

As the meeting came to an end, the room lit up with excitement, buzzing about the impending trip. Jonas strolled to his office.

"Mr. Rose, you have a visitor," Sandra informed him. "A Dr. Blake Sanchez is waiting in your office."

"Thank you, Sandra."

Jonas stepped into the office hand outstretched. "Good afternoon doctor, how's your day?"

"The best I've had all week!"

A hearty laugh encompassed them at the doctor's joke, being it was Monday the beginning of the week.

"That's a good one," Jonas said. "Did you get the invitation to our complimentary vacation?"

"Yes, I did, I look forward to it."

"So I can count you in then?"

"Of course, I wouldn't miss it for the world; it's just what the doctor ordered."

Again, they chuckled at the doctor's lighthearted wit. "It couldn't have come at a better time. I've had a good year; my financial advisor has saved me tons of money, so I'll be looking forward to treating myself real nice while I'm there."

"That's always good news, but you know this trip is all inclusive. Which one of our advisors are you referring to? I'd like to make sure and reward them for a job well done."

"Oh, she doesn't work for you, unfortunately."

"Maybe I know her, what's her name?"

"Samiyah Manhattan, that woman's a Godsend."

At the mention of Samiyah's name, Jonas was thinly coated in warmth.

"You know what I can do?"

The doctor looked on expectantly. "I can extend the invitation to your financial advisor. I'm feeling generous enough today, why not?" Jonas said.

"That is mighty thoughtful of you Mr. Rose. I'll be sure to inform her."

"You do that," he said all too content with his sudden luck.

"Hello, can I help you with anything today?" chirped the sales woman in the Victoria Secret lingerie store.

Samiyah answered with a gentle smile. "I'm not sure what I'm doing in here actually. I just finished getting a mani-pedi and all the pinks, reds, and yellow colors you have displayed in the store window caught my eye. I suppose a girl could always use a new panty and bra set."

The sales woman's eyes lit up. "I have just what you need. Follow me."

The woman guided Samiyah passed the different fragrances to an area of the store with panty and bra sets of all kinds. Getting a good look at Samiyah, the woman twisted her lips in thought.

"Let's see, if I had to guess, you look like a C-cup?"

"A very full-size C-cup," Samiyah offered.

"If you'd like to step into this dressing room, I can take your measurements, and we can get you in the perfect size. Believe it or not, many women don't wear the right size bra, but we've got you covered."

"Okay, let's do it."

They walked around the lingerie display tables to the dressing room, and Samiyah removed her top. The sound of India Arie rang out in the bottom of Samiyah's purse.

"Oh excuse me for a moment." Samiyah unzipped her bag, reaching past her bill folder, makeup kit, a couple of loose Benjamin's she'd just taken out of the ATM and clutched her phone. The incoming call came through her business line she swiftly answered.

"Samiyah Manhattan."

Hey, Samiyah, it's Claudia. You have an envelope here from Dr. Blake Sanchez. He stopped by the office, but I informed him you were taking personal time off."

"What is it?" Samiyah placed the phone in between her ear and shoulder and lifted her arms so the saleswoman could take her measurements.

"He only said it was a gift from him to you for doing such a fantastic job with his finances. Honey, he was cheesing so hard, with his cute dimples, and handsome self. I could've eaten him up standing right there in the lobby."

Samiyah rolled her eyes, "Girl, that is just too much."

"What," Claudia asked. "I need a doctor in my life, honey."

"That's what insurance is for, so you can get a good doctor," Samiyah chuckled.

"Oh ha, ha, you're very funny. Are you coming to pick this up or shall I keep it for myself?"

"Open it, and I'll let you know."

There was a rustling in the phone as Claudia opened the envelope and let out a sharp gasp. "Have mercy!"

"What is it?"

"An all-expense paid trip to San Juan, Puerto Rico!" Claudia's eyes almost popped out of their sockets.

"You're kidding."

"If I'm lying, I'm flying." Claudia gaped at the tickets in shocked disbelief. "He must have a thang for you. Who buys something like this as a gift unless they're interested?"

"I can't accept that; I'm sending it back." Samiyah quipped.

"You will do no such thing."

"I'm sending it back," Samiyah's tone was elevated and matter of fact.

"There's a note attached." More paper rustling, "Miss Samiyah Manhattan, please be so kind as to accept these two tickets to San Juan Puerto Rico. You can choose to bring anyone you like. The tickets are non-refundable so make sure to put them to good use. Signed, The good doctor."

Claudia squealed, "You must go! You heard the man, the tickets are non-refundable. Giving them back would be futile, and you can take anybody you want. It's not like he's asking you to take him. Besides, you've already got the time off, might as well take a trip."

Claudia had a point. Samiyah shut her eyes and wondered if she should give them back anyway. "Hold on," Samiyah put her top back on and stepped out of the dressing room, placing the phone back to her ear. "Do you want the tickets?"

"You know what, if I had the leisure to take some time off I would in a heartbeat because I can't stand this high and mighty attitude you're giving me, honey."

"I'm not giving you high and mighty, I just feel weird accepting a gift of that magnitude and why can't you take time off? Besides you know I volunteer at the hospital's NICU on the weekends."

"First, because you're already taking time off. Second, did you forget I'm my mother's primary caregiver? Trips like that have to be planned so that I can have the proper provisions in place. I would have to call my sister and make arrangements yadda ya. You know how this goes. Third, those precious preemie babies will be there for you to love on when you get back. Now stop coming up with excuses and take the trip!"

Samiyah sighed, "I'll be up there to get the tickets after I leave the mall."

Claudia cheered, "That's my girl."

"Have you picked out your dress for the March of Dimes benefit auction?"

"Yes ma'am, have you?"

"I think I'll pick out something when I get to Puerto Rico."

"You lucky, lucky girl."

They disconnected the call. Dr. Blake Sanchez was a very handsome man, with class and charisma, but she wasn't interested. Samiyah hoped for his sake this was truly a no strings attached gift.

Chapter Seven

"Ladies and gentlemen, we have arrived at San Juan Luis Munoz Marin International Airport. The local time is, one thirty p.m., and the temperature is eighty-seven degrees. For your safety, please make sure your seats are back and remain seated with your belts securely fastened.

When the Captain turns off the fasten your seat belt sign, we will have parked at the gate. This would be the best time to use your cellular devices if the need arises.

Make sure to check your area compartments for additional luggage, and please use caution when opening the overhead bins. On behalf of Southwest Airlines and the crew, I'd like to thank you for flying with us.

Enjoy your stay."

The seat belt sign disappeared, and Samiyah stood, stretching her arms. She had taken a fantastic nap on the way to San Juan. The day was young, and since she'd been coached into taking the trip, Samiyah planned to make the most of it. The airport hustled and bustled with many tourists, gatekeepers, police officers, and airport employees. Today, Samiyah wore a knee-length light blue and white sundress with white wedge heels. Her earrings, bracelets, and sunglasses matched her ensemble. As she made her way outside dragging her luggage on wheels, Samiyah passed vendors selling everything from suntan crèmes to t-shirts and handbags. Standing with a group of other men holding signs was her complimentary chauffeur. Samiyah strolled to the older gentleman holding *Samiyah Manhattan.*

"Hi, I'm Samiyah," she handed the man her I.D.

A polite smile lit up the man's face, and he bent slightly forward. "How are you today, Miss Manhattan?"

"I'm doing great, how about yourself?"

"Oh I'm splendid," he said giving her a flirtatious wink. "If you'll follow me this way, I'll lead you to your transportation." They walked to a limo, and Samiyah got in as he held the door open. In route, Samiyah mused about Jonas Alexander Rose. After she kicked him out, she never heard anything from him. It didn't surprise her, what did she expect? It wasn't like he knew her, but at the same time, she felt such a strong connection to him.

Too bad... Samiyah knew Jonas had moved on and never gave her a second thought. A resigned sigh escaped her. If she got the chance to see him again, she would let loose and have fun if only for one night. Samiyah tried to shake the pleasant thoughts away; she was getting herself worked up for nothing.   The limo pulled up in front of La Concha Renaissance Resort and parked. The chauffeur hopped out strolling quickly around to her door. He held his hand out, and Samiyah slid out one foot first.

"Thank you," she said.

"You're most welcome, enjoy your stay."

Samiyah handed the chauffeur a tip. "No thank you, ma'am, I've been compensated handsomely."

Again, he winked, and she gave him another thanks. Inside the resort, Samiyah checked in, received her key, and found the elevators. Being in the tropical island atmosphere lifted Samiyah's mood. She rode the elevator to her floor and entered the room. It was nicely designed with a king size bed, upscale fixtures, modern furniture, LCD TV's, and a patio overlooking the beach. Samiyah opened the doors and stepped out looking over the railings. With her nose in the air, her eyes closed, and a vibrant smile on her face she inhaled the exotic air. After having an appreciative look around, Samiyah placed her suitcase on the bed and opened it.

Before leaving Victoria Secret, Samiyah made it her mission to grab some swimsuits, and although she would go to the beach later, she wanted to find the hotel swimming pool now. Changing into her two-piece apple red bikini, Samiyah checked her reflection in the mirror. The sexy number was recommended by the same saleswoman who'd taken her measurements, and it fit around her breasts impeccably. The bottom half outlined her hips and cupped her butt, giving off a slight peek a boo effect.

Samiyah sat in a chair and used a natural shea butter crème to shine her feet, ankles, legs, and thighs. She worked the crème up her mid-section, rubbing it on her arms, hands, and fingers. Now she was glowing. Samiyah twisted her hair up using a pair of hair chopsticks to hold it in place. Grabbing her cherry blossom lip balm, Samiyah applied a coat of shine to her full lips. Taking another twirl in the mirror to check out her whole look gave Samiyah a satisfying grin. She headed out with a beach bag. When she found the pool area, Samiyah felt a thrill of pleasure. Claudia had been right; this is exactly what she needed. As she sauntered across the area, Samiyah found a lounge chair and sat down gracefully swinging her legs onto the extended furniture.

Leaning back, she rested her head and shoulders. In her beach bag, Samiyah pulled out a pair of sunglasses and a romance novel and began to read. After an hour, she put her book down for a moment and pulled out her mp3 player. She would listen to a couple of songs before taking a swim. Her focus was drawn toward a commotion at the entrance to the pool.

Heather Headley's 2008 neo-soul hit, "He is," wafted through her singular ear piece. Jonas strolled into the pool area with a cluster of women around him. He paused long enough to give a few autographs and pose to take a few selfies with fans. All of a sudden, Samiyah's throat went dry. What was he doing here, and most importantly, who was he here with?"

Samiyah's mind whirled as she thought about several possibilities for his attendance. Jonas looked from side to side and surveyed the area stopping dead center when his eyes met hers. *Lord in Heaven,* she thought to herself, this man was so deliciously designed. He took slow, deliberate steps in her direction and shed his shirt presenting a wide sexy chiseled torso. Samiyah could hear some of the women swoon as all eyes turned to his glorious perfection. Her heart beat raced, and she held her breath. Abruptly he stopped and pulled out his cell phone checking the caller ID.

Jonas answered the call, "Rose."

"Just the man I was looking for," Kevin quipped.

Jonas felt an annoyance, irritation, and frustration, none of which was displayed on his face. He kept his features neutral and continued to watch Samiyah as she rose to her feet beating a hasty retreat. Her beautiful brown body graciously glided across the cement surroundings of the pool, and she removed the chopsticks that held her hair in place allowing her tresses to tumble free past her shoulders down the middle of her back. The flick of her mane pushed back off her shoulders sent warm liquid coursing through his veins. Kevin was saying something about money being doubled for a fight. One thing Jonas had to give Kevin was his persistence, but Jonas was equally unrelenting.

"If this is about money just let me know, I'd be willing to help you out. How much do you need?"

A contemptuous scowl sounded through the speaker. "What?" Kevin said offended. "I'm not some charity case."

"You can work it off if that makes you feel any better, I have a job for you," Jonas offered.

Still, Jonas' eyes never left Samiyah. On the diving board now Samiyah leaped, bouncing twice; her body folding into a ball turning full circle before stretching her arms and legs out slicing into the water head first with the tenacity of an experienced swimmer.

"I've gotta go," Jonas ended the phone call and stepped out of his sandals making an unseen entrance into the pool. He watched her swim under water in his direction and wondered if her eyes were open. From his angle, he couldn't tell. Her long legs gracefully moved in waves like flippers behind her. When she came up for air, he got his answer. Samiyah thought she'd hit a brick wall when she collided with his broad chest. She opened her eyes, water dripping all over her face. Even in the cool water, the sight of him warmed her blood, and their collision caught her off guard causing her to grab hold of him.

"Jonas!" she breathed breathlessly. "I didn't see you." Her hand slid down his carved chest leaving a tingling in her fingers.

"That's because you had your eyes closed, love."

Samiyah blushed and attempted to take a step back from him, but his rough hands held her in place.

"What are you doing here, if you don't mind me asking?" It's not that she cared, she just wanted to know.

"I'm on vacation, you?"

"I was actually gifted this trip from a client, so," she held her arms out, "here I am."

Her radiant smile set a flame in him that dived right to the center of his groin. Never had he met a woman that set him ablaze like she did.

"Are you alone?"

"Yes, every time we cross paths I'm alone. It seems to be the story of my life."

He heard the sad undertone in her voice, and she looked away. With the tip of his fingers, he turned her back to him.

"That just makes me a lucky man."

Again, Samiyah blushed, her heart racing at his careful touch and sensitive words. "You're too nice; you don't have to say that."

"I don't say anything I don't mean, remember?"

She did remember.

"I don't play games, Miss Manhattan."

She held her hand up. "Please for the love of God call me Samiyah." To be clear she insisted, "at all times."

After Samiyah had spoken those words, she realized it indicated they would be together again. He caught it, too. A charming grin laced his handsome sculpted face. It was a good thing they were already wet, so Samiyah wouldn't have to worry about soaking her bikini bottoms.

"Have dinner with me."

Samiyah lifted a shoulder to her chin. Her head turned slightly, and her eyes lowered. "Was that a request or an order?" she batted her long thick eyelashes.

"That depends," he said closing what little gap was left between them. His torso touched her breasts and chills fled down Samiyah's skin.

"On what?"

"On how you like to be handled."

His breath danced across her lips like a stolen kiss. The fire between them crackled. Samiyah closed her eyes and inhaled his masculine scent. Their mouths were separated by a wisp of a breeze. Jonas reached for her.

"The water is boiling around you two, get a room!"

Samiyah's head whipped up; her eyes landing on a gorgeous, tall, delectable male. "Never mind him, that's my brother, Jaden," Jonas informed never moving an inch away from her. Now that Samiyah got a good look at him, he was one of the men on the front of the magazine cover. Of course, he was his brother. She remembered them all being strikingly handsome.

Her eyes traveled back to Jonas. "Good genes," she offered.

He cracked a smile, "Ditto."

His gaze held her in a deep sanctuary reeling her in with every second that passed. She swallowed back a lump in her throat.

"So tell me Samiyah, how do you like to be handled?"

Samiyah bit down on her lower lip driving him completely insane. "I guess you'll have to find out," she cooed letting her legs drop taking her underwater. She turned and swam off in the opposite direction, and Jonas swam after her, his sturdy arms catching her within seconds. He pulled her to the surface, twisting her around in his arms and Samiyah fell into a heap of laughter. Jonas pinned her against the pool wall and went under water placing his mouth on the softest part of her using his tongue to tease her most sensitive spot.

She gasped and shuddered trying to get out of his grasp, but her efforts were ineffective. "Okay, okay," she repeated. Slowly he gravitated above the water.

"What was that? I didn't hear you?"

She splashed him. "I'll have dinner with you."

Chapter Eight

The application of dark purple MAC lipstick left a smooth finish on Samiyah's lips. She puckered them and blew a kiss to herself flirting with her mirror image. So far, her day had been lovely. Running into Jonas at the swimming pool was the ultimate bonus. Even more blissful was the fact that he'd hung around for hours until Samiyah decided she was hungry. When he offered to buy her lunch, she declined and told him she needed to get something else done first. He had no idea her hunger had nothing to do with food. At first, she asked herself, what type of game was she playing.

It seemed as soon as Samiyah thought she could be carefree, she would close up and wonder if she was being reckless. Throughout her life, Samiyah had always kept things in perspective. She was never one to do things out of the ordinary for fear of what consequences would come from her actions. That didn't negate the carnal urges she buried deep inside her, for something adventurous, daring, and exotic in her life. Instead, she kept herself on remote; going through life business as usual. It was a true fight with self.

The black dress exquisitely adorned her physique, fitting snugly down her waist. It coiled around her bountiful bottom, and curvy hips; cutting into a slit down her left thigh. The dress stopped short midway, and Samiyah did a full turn in the mirror. She knew the dress was quite revealing, but she hoped to gain the attention of only one man tonight. With its thin material and light weight, the dress lay softly against her rich mahogany skin. She stepped into her dark purple five-inch stiletto's and decided to leave her clutch inside the room. She didn't want to carry anything but herself. Samiyah left the room making her way to the first floor. Music drifted from a nearby room drawing her attention. She followed the sound to an open area filled with people, food, and drinks. They talked, laughed, and danced with one another, some holding hands and others having flirty fun.

Gradually, Samiyah made her entrance, a clock on the wall read; 8:15 p.m., she was fifteen minutes late. She searched for him, strutting through the room using the poise of a feline. Men openly gawked at her; hypnotized by the racy sway in her hips as she made her way through.

"Miss Manhattan," a voice called.

Samiyah spun on her heels, bestowing a bright smile. She held out her hand to greet him. "Dr. Sanchez, hello, it's so nice to see you here." She really meant that.

The doctor assessed her, his eyes roaming from her dark flowing hair to the heels on her pretty feet. He accepted her greeting grasping her hand circling his thumb on her skin.

"You are stunning, Miss Manhattan. I'm glad you did use the tickets; it is well deserved," he said.

"Thank you very much. You're so kind; it is the best gift a girl could receive."

"Are you sure about that?"

Samiyah and Dr. Sanchez turned when they heard his voice. Jonas approached them in J Crew shorts, a crisp white button-down shirt that teased Samiyah with the two top buttons undone. It opened completely showing the long thick column of his neck then laid against his broad chest. He stepped into Samiyah's personal space and towered over her his eyes gleaming a wicked glow.

"Mr. Rose," the doctor sputtered. "I should've known it was you when all the women shifted to the other side of the room." He chuckled. "I was just telling Miss Manhattan here how delighted I am that she used the generous accommodations, you awarded her."

Samiyah frowned, "Um, the envelope was from you, Dr. Sanchez."

"Oh well yes, you see, Mr. Rose here paid for an all expense trip for his board members and contributors to his branch expansion opening up in New York City." The doctor's eyes uncomfortably shifted from Jonas to Samiyah. "I told him what a wonderful job you did helping me with my finances and he extended the trip to you as a reward for your outstanding service."

"Actually, I thought the gift was directly from you, doctor. Had I known it was from Jonas—"

"Then what? You wouldn't have come?" Jonas asked his voice calm and soothing. He slid his hands into his pockets and awaited her response. Jonas was ready to tear the dress off Samiyah she so effortlessly dangled in front of him; like a sheet over a masterpiece.

"What I was going to say is I would've acknowledged you instead. I was under the impression the gift was from the doctor."

"Sorry for the misunderstanding," Dr. Sanchez said. "If you'll excuse me."

He made his exit, embarrassed but delighted to get out of the hot seat.

"I must say Samiyah, you are the sexiest woman I've ever had the pleasure of laying eyes on."

Sudden warmth engulfed her, covering Samiyah's body like candy coated in chocolate. She blushed. "I'm flattered. Why didn't you tell me this trip was from you when you saw me at the pool?"

"You didn't ask."

She faltered, "But I asked you what you were doing here, and you said on vacation."

"It's true love, I'm on vacation. It didn't matter to me that Dr. Sanchez wanted to take credit for the trip. The only thing I cared about was getting you here." He spoke slow and sexy taking a step towards her.

"Why is that?" Samiyah stood facing him.

"I needed to check up on you. The last time I saw you, you were kicking me out."

She chuckled, "About that, I just needed some time to think. It was too much for me to process at once."

"There's no reason to explain. Samiyah... you get under my skin in a way I've never known. It's foreign, and I don't know what that means, but I want to find out."

The music changed and Floetry played. Samiyah took a labored breath, and Jonas reached for her enclosing his arms around her waist. He drew her in, and they slow danced as he kept his steely gaze fixed on her. They vibed and moved to the smooth melody.

"I hear congratulations are in order," Samiyah said.

He gave her a spectacular grin that spread his perfect lips showing a set of beautiful white teeth. "Thank you, we're looking to expand in more cities up north, and every time we do, we're taking a trip."

"It must be good to work for you." She let out a hearty laugh. He winked, and they swayed.

"I didn't want to leave you," Jonas said returning to the topic of her abrupt change in attitude the last time he saw her.

"Your sadness was overwhelming."

"I'm not sad now, quite the contrary actually," she smirked.

"Why is that, I wonder?"

"I think you know," Samiyah said.

"Why don't you tell me"

Samiyah wasn't willing to reveal that being around him made her feel like life would only get better. Jonas' hand ran up the back of Samiyah's neck into her hair. When he pulled her in, she let go, and they kissed. Soft, warm, and spicy, their lips caressed each other in a display of affection. Samiyah bit down on his lower lip, sucking it into her mouth. They're tongues mixed and mingled engaging in an erotic kiss that sent them shooting to the stars.

"If we keep this up," he said against her mouth, "Everyone is going to watch me make love to you right where we stand."

Samiyah kissed his lips again and backed away from him. He was making her delirious; her body a constant flame.

"Let me know who you are Samiyah. Tell me your hopes, your dreams, and desires."

"Excuse me," a woman stepped in between them. She looked to Samiyah. "Do you mind if I have a word with him?"

"Be my guest," Samiyah responded turning to make her way to the bar on the far-right side of the lounge. With the way Jonas had set her on fire, Samiyah was sure to leave a trail of smoke in her wake. He was irresistibly charming, and it was all she could do to keep from jumping his bones on the dance floor. Her emotions were on high, and although she'd come tonight to have fun, Samiyah couldn't control herself around him. He absolutely took her breath away. *Have fun girl, it's okay, it's not like you're going to fall in love.*

She took a look over at him. The woman was definitely a model; her tall, thin body leaned a shoulder into Jonas as she laughed about something that made him, in turn, react with an amused grin. Samiyah felt a slight tinge of jealousy and quickly turned back to the bar. The bartender approached her.

"Pinot Grigio, please."

The bartender left and came back with the white wine in no time flat. She sipped and tried to snuff out the flame that still sat at the core of her belly.

From across the room Jonas watched Samiyah intensely. She peeked over her shoulder and caught him staring at her. Samiyah's body language spoke volumes when she turned completely around raising her wine glass to her lips.

The owner of A Taste of Elegance Modeling Agency had interrupted their conversation, and Jonas was ready to pick back up where they left off. The woman laughed at her own comment leaning into him making sure to give him a full view of the cleavage that was about to fall out of her sequin top.

"I'm glad you ladies are having a good time, make sure to live it up while you're here," he said.

Samiyah sent him a flirty wink and a seductive smile beckoning him with her almond shaped eyes.

"Excuse me for a moment," he walked away, taking calculated steps like a man on the prowl. Other women tried grabbing Jonas attention as he neared, but they were out of his range of sight. The only thing he could see was Samiyah. When he pulled up next to her Jonas raised a finger and gave a quick whistle, the bartender glanced his way and nodded.

"What was that about?" Samiyah inquired.

"Adding you to my tab. While you're here anything you buy is complimentary, that includes everything. Let me feed you."

She wondered if he was implying food. Jonas reached for her hand linking their fingers. They sauntered toward the dining area of the lounge and got comfortable in their seats. Samiyah crossed her legs causing her dress to rise just above her thighs. Jonas dissected her movements. The server emerged, but they hadn't had a chance to look over the menus. He must've noticed the sexual chemistry that crackled between them because a smile flickered across his face and he raised a tentative hand.

"If you don't mind, I could suggest an entrée."

Jonas looked to Samiyah for her approval.

"By all means," she said.

"The gnocchi pasta is an Italian dish that's coated with our signature sauce, small pouches of potatoes and topped with refined mozzarella sauce. It comes on one plate, the idea being to feed each other out of the same dish."

He looked from Jonas to Samiyah to check for their consent. With a burning fire in his eyes, Jonas said, "We'll take it."

Chapter Nine

"I never asked you, what do you do for a living now that you no longer fight?"

"I took over my father's company, Rose Bank and Trust Credit Union. I was appointed the CEO and Chairman."

"So, you took over the company before you retired from boxing?"

He dipped his head in agreement.

"Is that the reason you put up your gloves?"

"No," was all he said. He turned the focus back to her, no doubt wanting to change the subject.

"It seems we have something in common, Samiyah."

"Which is?"

"Finances."

This time it was Samiyah who agreed with a nod, "This is true," she agreed. "I think we have more in common than finances. When we first met I heard you speak in French. Are you familiar with the language?"

Jonas noticed the empty glass that sat in front of her. He took the opportunity to change his tongue. In French he spoke.

"Would you like more wine, sweetheart?"

Delighted, Samiyah responded in the Indo-European language, "sûr."

"Excuse me," he said catching a server who was passing the table. Jonas was given immediate attention. "My lovely companion would like another glass of your Pinot Grigio, and I'll have a glass of scotch."

The server left hastily to make their drinks.

"How did you know I was drinking Pinot Grigio?"

"Because I watch your lips move every chance I get, and I saw you place your order."

Samiyah inhaled a sudden breath; her tongue tracing her lips like they had a mind of their own. Sure enough, Jonas watched the tantalizing dance; his eyes now smoldering.

"I'm fluent in Italiano, Español, Français, and English. My father constantly spoke to us about learning other dialects. 'If you expect to travel the world one day, son, then you better know how to speak the language,' he'd say." Jonas smiled as he reflected.

"So, we all took classes in grade school, and by the time we were in high school, those languages were just as fluent as English. With that being said my favorite of them all without a doubt is Français mi amour. It is by definition the language of love."

Samiyah wondered if she was literally melting right in front of him. Her insides were molten, and she could swear she smelled smoke. He licked his lips. "So tell me, when did you learn the lover's language?"

Samiyah was trying to hold it together. The last thing she wanted was to let him know how much he flustered her. "Much like yourself I learned in school, except my aunt was big on traveling, and whenever she'd come around, she spoke to us in a foreign language. If I talked to her in English, she'd ignore me until I spoke in French. It used to annoy me as a child, but I'm thankful for it now. I can't say that I'm fluent in anything else, but I'm sure you wouldn't mind giving me a few lessons." The fire that burned in his eyes officially engulfed her.

"I most certainly don't mind at all."

Needing to calm her raging hormones, Samiyah asked, "Did you travel alone or did you come with someone?" She realized that line of questioning wasn't ideal if she wanted to escape their flirtatious repartee.

Jonas drew her in with a charming smile. "I traveled with my brother Jaden. My employees came at their leisure."

"You have six brother's, right?"

"Yes, Jaden Jordan, Jonathon, Julian, Jacob and Josiah."

"The Rose Clan," she crooned.

A deep-set rumble of laughter left him. "That's what they call us."

"If you don't mind me asking, why does each of your names begin with J?"

"My father and mother had a rule. If they had boy's my pop would name us, if they had girls, my mom would. Our mother was the apple of my father's eye; he wanted to pay tribute to her by naming us all a name that starts with a J since her name is Janet. My mother did things a bit differently, whereas my three sisters hold my fathers middle and last name only. I used to watch my parents interact with each other and could tell their love was immeasurable."

The server appeared with their drinks.

"That's very sweet," Samiyah offered. "I didn't know you had sister's, too." She took a much-needed sip of her wine.

"Yes, three sisters, triplets, Eden, Phoebe, and Jasmine Alexandria Rose."

"Wow, that's a big family."

"You don't know the half of it. We're a true clan, hence the nickname."

"Your mother is a very lucky woman to have a man that loves her unconditionally.

"Yes, she was the love of his life."

Samiyah noticed the past tense and wanted to pry more but could feel the discomfort coming from him. Jonas reached for his glass and took a sip of his scotch.

"It's a shame real love doesn't exist like that anymore." Samiyah said.

With the conversation shifted to a lighter topic, Jonas' hazel eyes seemed to spark.

"Tell me," he said, "What happened?"

Samiyah knew exactly what he was asking. "Do you really want to know?"

"I do."

"David and I were high school sweethearts. In any competition we would win as a couple and were always voted most likely to succeed." Cruel laughter left her. "What a joke that was. We were young and in love. That's what I thought, anyway. He told me he didn't want to live without me and I believed him. We got married when I was twenty-three.

We couldn't afford the dream wedding I wanted, so we went to the courthouse. And we didn't get much of a honeymoon, more like a one night stay at the Holiday Inn. I didn't let that faze me; I was just happy and excited. I thought, we would be, most likely to succeed. But then not long after, he became distant and rude. I couldn't figure out where his attitude was coming from. I self-checked myself daily to make sure I wasn't fueling his anger, but it continued to happen.

Five years into our marriage I found out he was cheating. He was taking a shower and I'd decided to come home on my lunch break. His phone was on the counter, and it buzzed. I answered it without a second thought, and she asked to speak to him. I didn't automatically assume the woman was his lover until I told her he was showering and requested she leave a message."

Samiyah chuckled, "She called herself his fiancé." Samiyah shook her head. "I was so taken back by it that I checked out for a full sixty seconds. As you can imagine everything went downhill from there; I wasn't what he wanted. When it came to light, he didn't deny it. He never gave a reason why I wasn't enough for him or what changed. He just tossed me to the curb like trash."

Samiyah took another sip of her wine.

Jonas reached across the table, covering her hand with his. "I'm sorry. You know what they say," Jonas said.

"I'm afraid I don't."

He kept his focus on her eyes. "One man's trash is another man's treasure."

A nervous laugh chorused from her. "I don't know if I'll ever find out."

"And why is that?"

"I'm not putting myself on the market. I have no desire to go through the emotional stress of wondering, worrying, or hoping I'm doing everything I need to, to keep a man." Samiyah shrugged. "It's not worth it."

"Don't be so sure. I hope I didn't ruin your mood, but I need you to know David's a fool."

She blushed. "Don't I know it." They chuckled softly.

The server arrived with their food, steam rising from the plate. He produced two glasses of water with lemon.

"Enjoy," he sang, disappearing just as quickly as he came.

Jonas left his seat and occupied the seat next to Samiyah. His sudden closeness caused her nerve endings to stand on edge.

"Shall we pray?"

"Yes," she said.

"Jesus wept, Amen."

A burst of laughter drifted into the atmosphere. "Really?" she chorused, "That's all you got?"

"Don't judge me."

They laughed some more as he unfolded the cloth napkin that held the silverware wrapped tightly in an elegant display. He dug into the pasta twisting the fork holding one hand under the silver utensil as he fed her with the other. Her mouth opened and closed slowly around the fork sending a thrill of pleasure through him.

There was no way they were making it through this meal. Again, Jonas fed Samiyah, his libido losing its mind a little more with each lick of her mouth. Jonas remembered the sweet sauciness of the lips between her thighs and his carnal needs revved with want.

"You have something right here on your face, let me," he said leaning in to lick her chin up to the corner of her mouth. He captured her lips with his, and their tongues mated doing a dangerous salsa that made Samiyah moan into his mouth. She couldn't take it anymore, and neither could he. Jonas' hands explored her waist, back, and neck pulling her so close she was practically in his lap. Their kisses became heavy as they panted and tasted each other's flavor.

"I need you now." Samiyah said. "Now, now, now, now, Jonas."

Her begging was his undoing. He pulled away from her and rose taking her hand in his leading her out of the lounge. Jonas strides brought them to the elevator just as it dinged and opened. A group of ladies filed out, all giving Jonas a sexy glance. With purpose, Jonas stepped aside pulling Samiyah with him. He keyed in a code that would take them straight to the penthouse floor without making any pit stops.

When the doors closed, he turned to Samiyah lifting her by her bottom, her legs wrapping around his waist like it was natural to do so. Samiyah curved her arms around his neck, and Jonas placed her against the mirrored elevator glass wall. They devoured each other with Jonas leading a blaze of hot kisses from Samiyah's mouth to her neck and breasts. He grabbed the thin layer of material and ripped the dress from her glorified body. Samiyah yelped and salivated at the animalistic determination in his eyes.

Jonas feasted on her smooth skin working his way down her chest. With ease, Jonas lifted her higher as he got on bended knee. Samiyah's thighs sat on his broad shoulders, and she gasped holding on to his head with her back arched and shoulders propped against the elevator walls. Samiyah moaned when his tongue found the most delicate part of her. The sheer panties were no match for his skilled tongue. As they rose higher, the adrenaline that pumped through them was strong enough to make them run a marathon.

When they finally reached their destination, Samiyah was on the verge of an orgasm. Gently he eased her back down to his sturdy waist, and they kissed as he walked and carried her into his reservation. Jonas continued to the bedroom crawling on top of the king size mattress with her underneath him. Samiyah hurriedly helped him remove his button-down t-shirt revealing a sexy presentation of washboard abs.

He was so perfect and in the blink of an eye, Jonas no longer wore the cargo shorts. With her eyes on him,

Samiyah watched him discard his briefs. When he stood, she almost died at his girth. *My Lord in heaven.* He went to the bedside table and retrieved a condom wrapping his masculinity in front of her. As he crawled back on the bed, Jonas kissed her toes, ankles, and legs. He left a trace of steamy kisses up her thighs and smoothly removed her panties. Samiyah rolled to her belly.

"Will you unbuckle my bra straps, please?"

Her request was met with a naughty smack on her buttocks. She yelped, and her bottom bounced in response to his love tap. He unbuckled her straps, and kissed the round firmness of her backside. Samiyah threw the bra to the floor, and turned her head causing her hair to toss as she stole a look over her shoulder at him. She opened her legs inviting him to her love boat where she hid rocky waves and angry seas.

He met her back with tender warm lips sending a whirlwind of shutters up her spine. Jonas entered her from behind and Samiyah's mouth parted, opening wide at the immense intrusion. With each breath she took was an inch he gained inside her womanly core. Jonas' engorged erection was met with a waterfall of love that sealed him tightly like a matching piece of a puzzle. He started off slow and patient with the pace of a musician stroking the cords on a violin.

Jonas placed passionate kisses across Samiyah's shoulder blade, as he moved in and out, back and forth. Her moans became louder with each time Jonas drove into her. When Samiyah tilted her head sideways, Jonas stole kisses up her neck his tongue danced with her earlobe.

"Aaaaaah..." Samiyah trembled, and Jonas met her lips for an exotic masterful kiss.

One hand slid down her back to grip her waist with such a firm hold that Jonas was sure to leave fingerprints. He pulled her into him, her back arching and her bottom suspended in the air. Her knees trembled, and without warning, Jonas pummeled into her, his pelvis slapping against her ass, bold, heinous and headstrong.

She called his name, "Jonas..." Her voice sang in wrapped passion.

"Yes love, is this what you wanted?"

"Oui...oui..." she panted in French.

Jonas pulled out of her, flipping Samiyah over in one smooth motion to enter her from the front. On his way down to her breasts, Jonas stretched Samiyah's legs back as they came to rest on his shoulder blades. With his mouth to her breasts, he engulfed a nipple, sucking and teasing her brown areola, one after the other. Samiyah's head fell back, and she cried out to Jesus. His tongue lashed out, circling her heated skin as he penetrated her with monstrous strokes.

The room filled with their songs of praise as they both edged to the brink of their peak. Jonas' palms sank into Samiyah's skin tracing a path up her neck. He held on with a firm grip sinking sharp teeth into her flesh.

"Jonas!"

Her floodgates opened as Jonas rocked into her with supersonic speed. They made love for the better part of an hour, switching positions, going from the bed to the floor and back again. When Samiyah reached her breaking point, her shouts were garbled when Jonas sunk another powerful bite into her neck. With her body going into spasms, Jonas cupped her butt, lifting her closer to him as he drilled into her like a mine worker.

He whispered in her ear soft and slow, "You're all mine now, come with me, baby."

And she did. God help her soul. The orgasm was so fierce her entire body tingled with the sensitivity of a hot furnace. Right with her, Jonas release was just as powerful, and he grunted and groaned through the beautiful exoneration. He rolled them to the side, and they panted trying to catch their breaths. Samiyah looked over at him with awe. Where had he been all twenty-eight years of her life? She didn't have time to think about it before she drifted off into a restful sleep. Jonas watched her chest rise and fall in a quiet slumber. Samiyah was all he was missing and more. There was still much to learn about her, and he was ready to explore the debts of Samiyah Manhattan.

Chapter Ten

Samiyah's eyes fluttered open. A delighted smile creased her lips knowing instantly where she was. When she moved, the tight muscles in her thighs, legs and back told a story of their own. She was sore and rightfully so. Looking next to her the smile quickly turned into a frown. Jonas was gone. Samiyah swept her legs over the side of the bed and came face to face with a banquet of room service trays. She removed the top to the first tray and there lay a single red rose sitting on top of a note.

My love, I wish I could have been here when you awakened, but I am needed on a conference call. Please accept my apologies and enjoy your breakfast. The dress laying across the chair is a replacement for the one I destroyed last night. I would apologize for that, but, I'm not sorry. J. A. R.

Samiyah felt warm all over. She pulled the rose to her nose and inhaled lightly taking in the fresh fragrance of the beautiful flower. The breakfast trays were loaded with everything from bacon, eggs, grits, and potatoes to fresh fruit and orange juice. Although she wouldn't eat all of the food, it was fitting for her hearty appetite.

After breakfast, Samiyah thought about showering in his bathroom, but her essentials were still in her suite. For that reason, she decided to shower in her room. It only took her a minute to dress and make it to her quarters. Samiyah's thoughts never left Jonas. He made love to her like nothing she'd ever experienced. David was nowhere close to the passionate lover Jonas was, and Samiyah couldn't believe she'd been missing something so erotic all her life.

Jonas had taken her to new levels and how in the world would she move on from him to someone else? She didn't even want to think about it, but the reality was she would have to. Jonas was as unattainable as they come. With him being a celebrity, there was always a woman waiting in the wings to do or be whatever he wanted them to. Samiyah knew about his type, and there was no keeping a man like that. A moment of sadness fell over her but Samiyah quickly shook it off.

It's not like I'm trying to date anyway. That would be a total disaster, and it wouldn't be fair to him because he'd definitely be my rebound.

She reasoned with herself. This was just a weekend of fun. When she got back to work, things would go back to business as usual. After all, that was her method of operation. She finished her shower and stepped out wrapping herself in a towel. At the mirror, Samiyah wiped the glass trying to clear up the steam. She pulled the blow dryer off the wall and dried her hair. As she leaned to the side letting the heat dry her tresses, she combed through her thick soft mane with more thoughts of Jonas.

Samiyah had to snap out of it, and soon. Yeah, he'd put it down, but it was important that she didn't get lost in what was just a one-night stand. Jonas did say he's straightforward, right? If it's a fling, then it's a fling, she reasoned.

But he never said that about you.

Samiyah was driving herself half crazy. Hurriedly, she put on her clothes, grabbed her handbag, and left the room. She needed to put her mind on something other than Jonas, and she knew just what to do to accomplish that.

When the elevator reached the first floor, Samiyah made her way to the clothing boutique. A bell chimed as she entered the store.

"Hello, welcome to Johanna's Fashionista," a young Asian woman approached her. "Let me know if I can help you with anything."

"Actually, can you point me in the direction of your evening gowns?"

"My pleasure. If you tell me what the occasion is I can point you in the right direction. We have a plethora of different evening gowns, right down to cocktail dresses."

"It's a fundraising event, red carpet," Samiyah confirmed.

"Aaah, yes, step right over here."

The woman led Samiyah around some mannequins dressed in elegant evening gowns and spotted one that was strikingly beautiful. She floated to it touching the silk fabric.

"I see you've spotted one, you like. That one would be perfect for you. Would you like to try it on?"

Samiyah beamed, "Yes, I definitely would."

In the dressing room, Samiyah twirled around in the dress. Surely, she could get a bid with this ensemble on. The all white sexy spaghetti strap gown fit snugly opening down her back. The front held her breast up firmly in place showing an adequate amount of cleavage. From there the tightly fitted dress curved her apple bottom stopping right above her knees before sprouting into a thin layer of silk material that sat around her ankles. To say it fit perfectly was an understatement showing every curve that she owned. This was the one. She took out her phone to snap a picture and send to Claudia when she noticed the twelve missed phone calls.

Alarmed, Samiyah redialed Claudia and got an answer on the second ring.

"Tell me all about it!" Claudia shrieked, sounding excited about something Samiyah had no idea about.

"What are you talking about? I've got twelve missed calls from you; you tell me all about what's going on. Is something wrong at the office?"

"No, no, no," Claudia repeated. "You seriously don't know?"

Samiyah didn't have the slightest clue why her friend was so frantic. "I don't, what is it?"

"Girl what are you doing, hiding in a cave?"

"I'm standing in the dressing room in the gown I've picked out for the auction benefit. I was getting ready to send you a picture of it when I saw the missed calls. I don't know how my phone ended up on silent and I have no idea what you're blabbering about. Now can you stop beating around the bush and tell me what's going on?"

"Hold on," Claudia said. The phone went silent for a minute before Claudia came back to the phone. Samiyah's phone buzzed. "Okay check your text messages."

Samiyah pulled the phone away from her ear and opened her messages. She froze and her mouth dropped open. It was a newspaper clipping of the Chicago Tribune. It read;

"A blazing love affair for the most eligible bachelor, businessman, and former boxing world champion Jonas Alexander Rose?"

The clipping showed a picture of them last night on the dance floor in the most romantic embrace. Her hand was softly touching his chest, her face flushed with a demure smile lingering. The look on his face was adoring, sexy, and exotic and his lips were inches away from hers.

"Oh my God!"

On the other end of the phone, Claudia squealed, "You lucky, lucky girl!"

Inside the San Juan conference and business center, Jonas looked away from the detailed analysis report that displayed projections of key factors for Rose Bank and Trust Credit Union's next branch expansion located in New Jersey. He listened to Tim Harper from The Harper Group go over the report through a speaker phone sitting in the middle of the conference table. As the man spoke about, population, age distribution, per capita income, past household growth, among other things, Jonas' mind seemed to only be focused on one thing, Samiyah Manhattan.

It was common for him to meet a beautiful woman, take her to a hotel and rock her world before disappearing without so much as a trace of his scent left behind, but never had a woman gave the same amount of passion in return as he did. Besides that, he'd never had his thoughts dominated by a woman to the point where he couldn't focus on day to day business. It was true, Jonas didn't expect to be pulled into a conference while on vacation, but it had happened before, so he wasn't one hundred percent surprised.

However, when he woke that morning and gazed at the sleeping beauty next to him, his heart leaped, and wanted to stay enthralled around her. Jonas had a mind to plant kisses on her soft, delectable lips but there was no time. He slipped out of bed and made his way to the meeting after ordering her room service and having his assistant shop for a dress.

"That's good news," one of his board members shouted.

Jonas glanced at the members around the marble glass table one by one, his eyes landing on his brother Jaden who was staring at him intensely. Jonas leaned forward in his chair.

"Thank you, Tim, for that long, detailed report that could've waited until I got back in my office on Monday."

Everyone in the room snickered. "You know when we get the information we like to be prompt with our findings," Tim said.

"I know, I know," Jonas repeated, "I'm just giving you a hard time."

"I'll let you get back to it. Look to hear from you on Monday," Tim said.

"You got it."

The called ended and members of the board shuffled around gathering their papers, filing out of the room. As they exited, Amanda Davis, Jonas' assistant entered the room handing him a copy of the Chicago Tribune. There he was front and center with the woman that riddled his thoughts. Whoever the cameraman was had taken an ideal shot of them, and they looked like a couple in love. It didn't surprise him; there was nowhere Jonas could go that would keep paparazzi from getting a shot of him. Except for Terrance's back home in Chicago.

"It's in every major newspaper across the country." Amanda spoke flatly.

She didn't sound too enthusiastic about it. Truth be told, after going through stringent background checks, drug tests, and health screenings, Amanda was delighted when Jonas chose her six years ago as his assistant. She had the same hopes as many women who applied for the job; to show hard work and one day possibly be chosen as his love interest. Amanda had sat on the sidelines and watched as Jonas was with one model after the next, but they never lasted long, and in her spirit, she hoped this latest one wouldn't either.

"Thank you, Amanda, anything else?" he spoke disarmingly.

Reluctantly she replied, "No sir, that will be all." Amanda went towards the door then turned back suddenly. "I'm going to lunch would you like to accompany me?" She held her breath, when he didn't respond quick enough she said, "Or I can grab you something if you're hungry."

He was hungry. He'd left for the meeting this morning without eating breakfast, and his tank was running on empty.

"I think I will."

Jonas rose from the swivel chair. Amanda gleefully smiled.

"Give me just a moment," Jonas said. He turned to Jaden who'd been watching him all morning. Amanda closed the door leaving them alone in the conference room.

"What can I help you with little brother? Looks like there's something on your mind," Jonas said.

"I was just thinking the same thing about you. How's it going with Samiyah? I see you managed to get her here."

"Get her here? I don't know what you're talking about."

Jonas said it with a straight face. Jaden gave an incredulous grin, "I think you do."

When Jonas didn't respond, Jaden laughed slapping him on the arm.

"You're good. She is gorgeous, stunning, actually. Since you're not interested, maybe I'll try my luck with her. Seems like my kind of woman," he winked.

Jonas crossed his arms over his extensive chest with a look of dare in his eyes. "Go right ahead, if you want me to ball you up like I used to when we were kids, the difference being I'm a little bigger than that one-hundred and twenty-pound middle schooler you use to know." Jonas grimaced showing no signs of a joke.

"That's what I thought," Jaden said chuckling. He stuffed his hands in his pockets, whistling on his way out the conference room.

Chapter Eleven

Samiyah dialed Jonas' penthouse suite and waited patiently for him to answer. When he didn't, she hung up and redialed the number. No answer. Samiyah huffed.

The newspaper clipping disturbed her. She was a professional for Pete's sake, on the front page looking like she had a school girl crush. Samiyah went in search of Jonas stopping by the conference rooms first. He did say he had an urgent call to take, so maybe he would be there. When she reached her destination, to her dismay, Jonas was nowhere in sight. Samiyah let out an exasperated sigh.

When I'm not looking for him, he'll show up.

She was right. The hotel was huge; it could take all day to find him. Maybe she should just plan her day out and wait to run into him.

But what if you don't?

Samiyah groaned. It was 1:48 p.m., today she would make it her business to get to the beach. This was a four-day three-night trip, and there was much to explore. Deciding to get something to eat, Samiyah made her way to Delicias, a restaurant inside the hotel.

On her way, Samiyah received pleasant smiles and flirtatious looks from women and men alike. In her mind, she wondered if they recognized her as the lovesick woman on the front of the newspaper.

Stop worrying about something you can't control.

When she made it to the restaurant, Samiyah sauntered to the first free table she saw. It sat by glass windows with a view of the palm trees and beautiful blue waters that surrounded them. The feel of the restaurant was busy, the décor upscale, and no one seemed to be sitting alone but her. As she waited for a server to approach, Samiyah got lost in her thoughts. It wasn't long before the waitress manifested to take her order. Looking over the menu, she placed an order for grilled chicken quesadillas and a glass of water.

As the waitress walked away, Samiyah eyed her movements which came to a halt when she passed him. A rush of emotions filled her gut. There Jonas sat, comfortably in simple but sexy attire. Her eyes zeroed in on his face. He lifted a fork to his mouth, and Samiyah caught herself softly moan. It was barely above a whisper.

Then his tongue licked his delicious lips, and he took another bite of his food. Samiyah envied that fork. A charming smile broke out sitting high on his masculine face. It was followed by a burst of laughter and a nod of the head. It was then that Samiyah realized he had a companion. From her long slender legs, Samiyah knew she was tall. Her brunette hair was in a bunch of curls that curved her ears. Samiyah was unable to see the woman's face, but from a distance, she could see enough.

A pang of jealousy ran through her core. Samiyah tried unsuccessfully to dismiss the feeling. It was uncomfortable and confusing. She didn't want to care. There was so much she didn't know about Mr. Jonas Alexander Rose, and Samiyah wasn't trying to find out.

What did she expect, he was Chicago's most eligible bachelor after all. When paparazzi got a hold of a picture of him today, they would forget all about her. *Yes*, Samiyah reassured herself. So why on earth did she care so much?" Another beat passed, and he looked over meeting her quizzical stare.

Now her heart was racing double time, and she quickly looked away. Clearing her throat, Samiyah placed her focus outside the glass window and held it there.

When Jonas saw her, there was an unfamiliar leap in his chest that confused him. The broad smile that sat on his face dissipated. He wondered how long she'd been watching him. Dr. Blake Sanchez entered the room seeing Samiyah immediately. The doctor strolled to her table. Jonas watched as he interrupted her thoughts. A look of surprise catching her face. The doctor spoke, and a gorgeous smile lit up her beautiful expression.

Again, there was that leap in his chest. Samiyah shook her head yes and the doctor took a seat across from her. The waitress appeared with her food and took the doctor's order.

When she began to eat Jonas' mind flashed back to memories of her delicate lips on him; licking softly across his neck, biting down on his shoulder, kissing up his jaw and nibbling on his ear. When she took another bite, her eyes met his and this time she licked her lips.

"Excuse me."

Jonas was up moving towards her like a predatory animal. Samiyah took a sip of her water to calm her nerves. When Jonas approached, he could hardly take his eyes off her.

"Good afternoon, Samiyah," Jonas glanced at Dr. Black Sanchez. "Doctor," he said quickly acknowledging him.

"Jonas," the doctor said, surprised once again by his sudden appearance. "How are you today?"

"I'm well," he responded to the doctor, but his eyes lingered on Samiyah. She took another sip of her water.

"Good afternoon, Jonas," Samiyah said. "Enjoying your lunch?" A smile dashed across her lips.

Jonas slid his hands into his pockets. "I did, I missed breakfast this morning, and I was in desperate need of a bite to eat after working up such an appetite last night." He spoke low; his voice, deep.

Samiyah swallowed hard.

"You work too hard," the doctor chimed in, "even on vacation. How do you plan to relax and take a load off," he asked.

"I've got an idea," Jonas said, speaking to the doctor but sending a direct implication toward Samiyah.

The doctor laughed, "I'm sure."

"Samiyah, do you mind if I speak to you for a moment?"

"Actually, I do need to have a word with you. Dr. Sanchez, you don't mind if I speak to Mr. Rose for a minute, do you?"

"Of course not, take your time."

Samiyah rose from the table and walked passed Jonas exiting the restaurant. When they got outside, she turned to him.

"Did you see the Chicago Tribune, today?"

"I did."

He stepped closer to her. Jonas had a thing about getting into her personal space. Samiyah let out a deep breath to refocus her thoughts.

"Well, what are you going to do about it?"

Jonas lifted a brow. "What's wrong with it?"

She crossed her arms. "Are you serious? They think I'm your love interest."

"I'm waiting for the part where this should be an issue for us."

Did he say us?

"The problem is, I'm not your love interest. Look, I've got a career, and I'm still building my client list. I can't have people thinking I'm one of your one hit wonders."

A silly smile cracked Jonas' lips replaced by a humorous laugh. He was so irresistibly charming she couldn't help but laugh, too.

"This isn't funny, Mr. Rose."

He reached for her, drawing Samiyah into his embrace. "But you're laughing." Her head fell forward landing on his chest as she let out a cheerful laugh.

"And since when did we go back to referencing each other with a formal address? I think we're more than acquainted enough to be on a first-name basis."

Pulling back from him, Samiyah looked into his eyes. It was amazing how she felt just being here with him.

"I don't assume anything, Mr. Rose." He gave her a stern look. "Okay Jonas," she said taking back the formality.

"You don't have to, always call me Jonas."

Always?

"How was your breakfast," he inquired.

"It was fabulous, thank you."

"You're more than welcome. Listen, if you have a problem being photographed with me, tell me what to do, and I'll do it." He was being serious. "I don't want you to think being with me will ruin your reputation or the reputation you're trying to build. I would never want to put you in that position."

His face was so close just an inch more, and her lips could touch his.

"Hey, Mr. Rose, sorry to interrupt, I took care of the check, and I'm off to the beach if you need me."

Samiyah pulled slightly away from him.

"You did use the company card, right?"

"Should I have," Amanda asked.

"Whenever you're on company business, you use the company card."

"I did, I'm just playing around." A shy laugh departed from Amanda before extinguishing into an artificial smile.

Jonas smiled brightly. "Samiyah this is Amanda, my assistant. She's dealt with me for six years now. A real trooper, I hope she stays around for a while. It would be hard to replace her." Amanda gushed. "Amanda this is Samiyah Manhattan," he paused then said, "My love interest."

Chapter Twelve

"Do you have any plans tonight?"

"No, I've done what I needed to do today," Samiyah said.

Jonas grabbed her hand threading their fingers together. Samiyah's heart skipped a beat.

"Take a walk with me, love."

He started out of the hotel with her, hand in hand. Outside, the sun shone brightly with high blue skies. Jonas covered his eyes with aviator sunglass, and Samiyah pulled a sun hat from her beach bag and placed, it on her head. As they strolled, Jonas put his free hand inside his pocket.

"Have you ever been here before, Samiyah?"

She pursed her lips. "I can't say that I have. It's a beautiful island."

"You haven't seen the half of it."

"What made you choose this as a destination?"

"When I was a kid, my brothers and I along with my father and mom would vacation here during the summer seasons. It was where they got married and spent their honeymoon."

"Sounds like a very happy childhood."

A sparkling grin covered his face, "It was."

"Are you the oldest of your brothers?"

"I am, and because of that, my father made sure I was the toughest. He made me set the tone for my younger brothers. They would always want to follow me around, and they kept a close eye on me. We were thick as thieves. You know how siblings are."

"I'd be remiss to say that I do." A grim look came over her. Jonas stopped walking and faced her.

"Are you an only child?"

"Yes, but it has its perks, I guess." A faint smile took over departing just as quickly.

Jonas touched her face, the palm of his hand caressing her cheek. "That's nothing to be sad about. I can imagine being the only kid. Your parents must've spoiled you to death."

"My parents were divorced by the time I turned four-years-old."

"I'm sorry to hear that."

She shrugged, "It is what it is, I guess. My birth was hectic; it was unlike the usual happiness that comes along with having a baby. My mom used to talk about it all the time. When her and my father found out they were having me, they were both immediately excited. But I came early, too early at 30 weeks. I ended up staying in the hospital for months until I was in better condition to go home.

Needless to say, I have a soft spot for preemies. Every weekend I try and dedicate my volunteer services at the local hospital's neonatal intensive care unit." She smiled sheepishly, "Except for this weekend of course. You have my best friend to thank for that."

"I'll make sure and thank her," he said.

"Anyway, taking care of me came with its own set of challenges. For one, I came home on oxygen, and I had a few delays with crawling and walking. My parents would often argue, mostly my dad, who felt my mother wasn't helping me enough." A smile dotted her face but went away before it could fully form. "Then the weekend of my birthday, I saw my mom crying her eyes out in the kitchen. I asked her what was wrong and she tried to pretend she was okay. She didn't tell me that day, but eventually, she did."

"My dad remarried and moved to Atlanta with his wife. I didn't see him for years until I was nineteen. By then, the memories I had of him were vague. He would pop up every couple of years and take me to dinner, or buy me a car; sometimes he would send money. He ended up having two other kids, and I never saw them. Then one day, my mom pulled up in front of the house and asked me to come outside. When I got in the car, I could tell something was wrong."

Samiyah looked off into the distance. "That's when she told me that he'd had a massive heart attack." Samiyah's eyes watered and she flickered an invisible piece of lint off her shoulder. Quickly she swiped her eyes. Jonas drew her in, his arms circling her for protection. She tried to compose herself but was too far gone to stop the trail of tears that stained his shirt. He felt her body vibrate and kissed the top of her head holding on to her for dear life.

"He passed away. The doctor's said his brain went without oxygen for too long before help arrived." More tears ran down her face, and she cried audibly.

"I'm so sorry, sweetheart." Jonas stroked her back and kissed her forehead, his hold never wavering.

She allowed him to cuddle her and relaxed against him. Although she'd cried when it happened, Samiyah never expressed how she felt about the whole ordeal. After another minute, Samiyah straightened herself enough to calm down.

"I'm sorry about that," she said shyly.

"There's no reason to apologize. I can't help but feel that you blame your early birth for your parents' separation. But you shouldn't. That is on them, not you."

"I'm sure you're right, and I've never shown anyone how I felt."

"Not even your ex?"

"Especially not him. He would just say, what are you so sad about? It's not like you really knew him."

She shrugged, "In a way he was right, but it didn't mean I didn't love him and it hurt that he died without me having the chance to have him in my life." She wiped her eyes.

"I'm sorry to hear that. I feel privileged to be the shoulder you cry on."

"You said you and your brothers were thick as thieves, are you not anymore?" Samiyah was happy to change the subject.

Following her lead, Jonas slipped an arm around her shoulder and they proceeded to walk down the beach.

"We are still close; we're just grown now and have our own endeavors. We all own our own businesses, and Jaden is the brother I see on a regular basis. He's an investment banker. My right-hand man."

"What about your parents," she asked. There was a fleeting look of despair that crossed his face.

"My father Christopher Lee Rose is retired. He lives in Chicago in a home big enough to house us all, with our housekeeper, Norma. He won't get rid of it because it holds so many memories. I swear he thinks one day we'll all move back in."

He chuckled. "Before he retired, my father purchased Gemz."

"The chewing gum company?" Samiyah asked.

"Yeah. I thought he wanted it as a side hobby, but then he told me, the purchase had everything to do with Josiah, my younger brother. Right now, Josiah is the only one of us that doesn't own a business, but he's in his prime and holding a steady gig as a top salesman at Infiniti."

"So your father plans to give him the company?"

Jonas smirked, "I wouldn't say give. Josiah will have to work for it. I'm not sure exactly what my father has up his sleeves. But whatever it is, Josiah will have to compromise to get it." Jonas stopped walking and turned to Samiyah. "Let's do something fun." He said suddenly.

She smiled joyfully, "What did you have in mind?"

"Follow me."

Grabbing her hand, Jonas led Samiyah back to the hotel and into the casino. Sounds of slot machines dinged, music played, and people cheered as they tried their luck with various games. Waitresses walked around with trays displaying white and red wine.

"I'm not dressed for this." Samiyah halted.

Jonas looked Samiyah over; she was wearing a sleek purple sundress that hung loosely to her mid thighs. Her flip flops were black with purple flowers and remnants of sand sat in between her toes.

"I think you look absolutely beautiful."

Samiyah gazed into his hazel brown eyes and almost lost herself. She removed the sun hat and stuffed it back into her beach bag, finger combing her hair. With one swipe over her shoulder, her hair hung to the side. Jonas loved it when she flicked her hair like that. It was becoming his favorite thing. He licked his lips.

"Mr. Rose," someone yelled. One after another, heads turned their way. Some people pulled out their cell phones and took pictures from a distance while others flat out recorded them.

With her hand still in his, Samiyah squeezed tightly as the barrage of people crowded around them. Was this what it would be like to be with him on a regular basis? She didn't like it one bit. It was too overbearing and suffocating.

Well, it's a good thing this will only last the weekend.

Samiyah felt a bit of sadness at that thought, but she had to keep her mind straight even if her heart was trying to tell her something else.

Jonas slipped a look at her and saw the uncomfortableness in her demeanor. "Are you okay?" he asked. "If you want to leave we can go."

She exhaled a deep breath and braved the crowd, pulling Jonas through the onslaught of people snapping pictures and trying to get an autograph. They pulled up short to a craps table and watched as the dealer turned the hockey puck to 'OFF.' A guy standing at the front of the table placed his bet, twenty thousand. He picked up the dice and shook enthusiastically then yelled out, "Daddy needs a new pair of shoes," before throwing the dice down. All eyes followed the pair as they rolled to a slow stop landing on a combined three points.

"Awe!" The crowd cried, and the dealer secured the man's chips.

"Daddy needs another drink now." The man mumbled walking away from the table. The crowd laughed, and another man stepped up. When he rolled, one dice landed on a seven while the other took a second to fall flat on a five.

"Oh come on!" he yelled losing his ten thousand. A waitress approached Jonas with a tray of chips.

"Mr. Rose, these are complimentary from the owner." The woman smiled and winked never giving Samiyah a second thought.

"Complimentary?" Samiyah said. "Impressive. Do people always give you whatever you want?"

A superior smile adorned his lips. "Always." His brows jumped, and she laughed. The sound of her delightful voice sent shivers through him and that tug he'd felt all day was back. Jonas put his hand in hers and guided her to the top of the table. The dealer turned the hockey puck to 'OFF,' and Jonas took the fifty thousand dollars worth of chips and sat them all on the table placing his bet.

Incredulously Samiyah said, "All of them?"

Jonas smirked and grabbed the dice juggling them back in forth in his hands. He held them up to her lips.

"Blow," he said. His words sent a tremble down her spine. As Samiyah watched him watching her, she leaned in close enough to kiss his fingers and blew softly. The wind from her lips set his fingertips on fire, and his eyes sparkled. Absentmindedly, he tossed the dice across the table but kept his eyes on Samiyah. There was a tense silence around the table before the crowd went wild yelling, SEVEN! Jonas was awarded another fifty thousand dollars, but while everyone cheered around them, Samiyah and Jonas were still stuck in the depths of their captivating gaze where no one belonged but them.

Chapter Thirteen

The day went on with Jonas and Samiyah making two hundred and fifty thousand dollars. Every time they won more, Jonas would put it all on the table and Samiyah would take half of it away.

"If you keep this up I'm going to have to appoint myself as your financial advisor," she would say.

He'd laugh at her. "Money is no object, my love."

"Un huh, we'll see if you're singing that same tune when you're sixty-five going into retirement."

"By then I'll have enough to take care of a village for the rest of our lives." He was giving her that piercing stare again making her stomach flip flop.

What was this OUR business he mentioned, she wondered but tried not to look too deep into it.

Finally, they cashed in their chips. At the window, the lady asked him how he'd like his winnings. He asked her for a pen and a piece of paper. She handed him a notepad with the casino's logo on the front and an ink pen with the same logo. He wrote something down and slid it back to her.

"As you wish," she smiled delightedly.

He turned to Samiyah, "I want you to see something. The night is still young, would you mind spending a little more time with me?"

"Not at all," she responded affably.

Jonas led her out of the resort to valet. The young man approached him, "On second thought." Jonas said getting her undivided attention, "You might want to grab a change of clothes."

Samiyah lit up with curiosity. "Why would I need a change of clothes?"

He smiled a devilish grin, "because where we're going, you're going to get wet."

Uncontrollable heat ran throughout her, festering around her center. She gave him an untamed look. "Well I'm wearing my bikini underneath this dress, so in that case, I could just remove my clothes and leave them in my beach bag."

His gaze was now piercing her soul; he ran a slow examination from her head to her toes; the thin material doing nothing to hide her womanly curves. Slowly, his tongue traced his bottom lip, and he bit down tightening his jaw. Valet stood there watching the exchange, and a small grin appeared on the man's face. Jonas gave the valet a ticket, and he happily ran off.

Three minutes later a Ferrari California pulled to the curb. It's black shiny exterior gleamed in the nightlight. As she sauntered up, Samiyah couldn't help but have an appreciation for the sports car. The top was down showing the Ferrari's red leather interior which gave it an air of spunk. Jonas opened the door for her, and she slid in. Samiyah gave an approving glance over the car and wondered if it was his vehicle.

They pulled off and cruised onto the nearby highway.

"Is this your car?" She had to know.

A mischievous grin covered his face. "It is."

"Do you have a different car everywhere you go?"

"As I said, I've been coming here for years; this is like a second home to me. So, of course, I have more than one vehicle and a house on the beach."

Her eyes rose in surprise.

"Would you like to see it?"

That grin was still on his face.

"Sure," she replied coyly.

Jonas tried to keep his eyes on the road, but it was getting harder by the second. Being with Samiyah felt so right to him, and Jonas wanted to keep her around him as long as she would permit.

"Why are you staying at the resort?" she asked.

He leaned her way resting his elbow on the middle console. "I wanted to be where you are."

She gave him a sultry look her eyelids faltering. Since she'd been with him, Jonas said things that kept her wondering. Samiyah didn't want to jump to conclusions, but he was making it hard for her. It could've been as innocent as, I wanted to make sure you got here safely or I wanted to welcome you to San Juan.

But that's not what he said.

Samiyah had to remind herself that she shouldn't overthink it constantly. She shouldn't even care. Samiyah hadn't been divorced for a month. To have such thoughts was ridiculous. She looked down at his hand on the gear shift, smoothly shifting with ease. His other hand lay languorously on the steering wheel.

"Did you bring a change of clothes?" she questioned him.

"I don't mind getting a little wet," he said with a wink.

Samiyah crossed her legs and shifted in her seat. Jonas watched her movement. "Are you okay?" his baritone voice slid over her body like a second skin coating her with a warm heat.

"Yes."

His lips spread into a thin smile and he shifted gears. They pulled up to Las Cabezas, a fishing village found on the northeastern tip of Puerto Rico. Parking and exiting the Ferrari, they made their way to the beach. When they approached, an Eco adventure guide moved toward them.

"Hey Jonas, it's been a little while."

Jonas smiled holding his hand out for a shake.

"It has, hasn't it?"

"I'd say about four years."

"Has it been that long?" Jonas inquired.

"I'd say so."

"I don't always have a reason to stop by."

The man looked to Samiyah then back to Jonas, a broad smile sitting high on his face. "I see you do now."

"This is Samiyah Manhattan, Samiyah this is George. He's been the guide here for over ten years now."

"Hello," Samiyah said shaking George's hand.

"Step over here, Miss. Manhattan."

"Please call me Samiyah."

"Alright, Samiyah it is," George said.

"What are we doing exactly?"

"We're putting on gear to go kayaking."

"In the dark?" she questioned.

"You're not scared, are you?"

"That would have to be a yes."

Jonas chuckled. Samiyah held an incredulous scowl on her face. He reached for her chin his hand caressing her pout.

"Do you trust me?"

"What does this have to do with trust?"

"It has everything to do with it."

The Eco Guide handed him a life jacket, rope, a whistle, and a night safety light. He pulled Samiyah to him putting on the life vest snapping the buckles snuggly. After securing his jacket they made their way to a kayak, and Jonas helped her in.

"Don't worry; you're in good hands," Jonas assured her.

The lights on the kayak illuminated. Slowly Jonas started to row. They headed towards a hidden opening in the mangroves at the northern end of the beach. Once there, he rowed for a mile taking them to Laguna Grande. Samiyah gasped at the breathtaking scenery. The lagoon spread into a wide span of flowing water enclosed around a mangrove woodland. Mountains sat in the distance along with a waterfall.

"Wow," she said.

The kayak floated smoothly through the dark waters. "The lighthouse on the left was built in the 19th century, but that's not what I wanted you to see."

He reached forward and shut off the lights on the boat, putting his paddles gently back in the water. Suddenly, the kayak around them lit up with an iridescent glow.

Samiyah gasped again clutching her chest. The sight was more beautiful than anything she'd ever seen.

Jonas moved closer to her. "Those are bioluminescent plankton." He moved the row, and they continued to glow like a twinkling sky. He put an arm around her cuddling her close to him. Those were not the safety rules for the kayak, but he couldn't help himself. Samiyah leaned into him, allowing herself to be comforted in his embrace. They moved softly and quietly through the water the plankton lighting a trail as they passed.

"Did you come here often as a kid," she asked.

"Every chance we got, which was whenever we traveled here."

"This is amazing, thank you for showing me this."

"You're more than welcome, I figured you'd like it."

"You figured, huh?"

He chuckled, "I'm glad I was right."

She gave him a warm smile. "That you definitely are." And he was too right. Being with Jonas was becoming something she thoroughly enjoyed.

"Promise me something," she said.

"Anything."

"We'll always be friends."

She leaned her head back to look up at him. His eyes were intense and steady. His arms tightened around her waist. They both felt more than friendly for each other, but neither one was willing to admit it. Jonas kissed her on her forehead down to the tip of her nose then moved to her lips. She closed her eyes letting the heat from his mouth coat her in a delicious wave of euphoria.

Their kiss seared, Samiyah biting down on Jonas' lips, pulling and licking not missing a beat. Soon audible moans could be heard coming from both of them as Jonas turned her towards him. The kayak bobbed and rocked slightly with water creeping over the edges soaking them from the waist down. They paid it no mind as their kiss turned into a fiery passion. Samiyah made an attempt to unbuckle her lifejacket tugging at it to no avail. Jonas pulled back from her.

"Are you sure you want to come out of this?" his voice was rugged and profound.

"I trust you," she spoke with bated breath. Her words sent a thrill of desire running through him. He unsnapped the jacket as if it was second nature. When it fell to the side, she removed the sundress revealing a two-piece bikini set that put her curvaceous body on full display. He gritted his teeth and removed his lifejacket and his t-shirt. Samiyah nibbled down on her lips and reached for his pants unzipping them slowly filling her hand with his girth. There was no way she could get used to his distended size. Samiyah pulled it out of his pants and moved her hand up and down his length.

"Take off your clothes." He commanded. She did what she was told slipping out of the bikini top and bottom. He removed a condom from his pocket and wrapped himself. He grabbed her hips lifting her like she weighed nothing. She folded her legs back as he sat her on top of him. Her arms curved around his neck.

When they connected, her mouth fell open, and desire rippled through her core. Samiyah's movements were slow but urging. Her head fell back as she lifted her hips up and down.

Every time the kayak moved, the waters around them lit up from the bioluminescent plankton surrounding it. Jonas encased Samiyah, his arms laying firmly around her with a fierceness that glued them together. Samiyah moaned and chanted for him to never let her go. His heart throbbed as they made love under the glow of moonlight surrounded by starry waters. He kissed her neck and sucked her breasts then made his way back to her lips. They rode into an orgasm so deep the kayak almost flipped from their shudders. They breathed heavy against each other's skin their eyes plastered to their faces.

"I'm not done with you yet," Jonas growled.

"I don't want you to be." She said.

They kissed again then slowly covered themselves as Jonas rowed back to the dock.

Chapter Fourteen

The immense size of Jonas' beach house sat behind a tall wrought iron gate. When he pulled up, an electronic voice rang out.

"Good evening, do you have an appointment?"

Jonas spoke into the receiver, "Jonas Alexander Rose."

"Good evening Mr. Rose, I hope you enjoyed your day, welcome home." The gate opened inward allowing them to pull through. He pulled around a circled driveway and parked in front of the door. Jonas stepped out of the Ferrari California and strolled around to the passenger side opening the door for Samiyah. He held out a hand helping her out of the luxury vehicle.

Taking a look at the huge home Samiyah gave him a side eye. "Are you sure you're not hiding a family inside this castle?"

He grinned, "Not yet." His gaze lingered on her for what seemed like forever.

"So, Chicago's most eligible bachelor does want to settle down one day?"

Jonas reached for Samiyah, drawing her into him. "Are you asking me to settle down?" His voice was low and profound.

Laughter like an angelic enchantress bellowed from her. The sound captivated Jonas' senses causing his body to react with unrestrained hunger. It was the most titillating melody he'd ever heard. No woman's laugh had ever made him so aroused to the point of fascination. Jonas brought his mouth down feasting on Samiyah's moist lips. Abruptly, her amusement turned into pleasure, she craved him just as much as he did her and their appetites for each other took over. Their tongues danced caressing the concave of their mouths with a heated and fiery passion that ignited an insatiable desire.

Jonas swept her up into his arms and carried her over the threshold. Samiyah's hands lay gently on his face, and they continued to kiss with Jonas never breaking his stride. Once they were in front of the fireplace, he laid her down on the large bear rug that lay neatly in front of it. With the flick of a button, the flames rose covering already chopped wood that sat ready to be burned. With only the glow of fire creating shadows that bounced off the walls and furnishings, Jonas removed his clothes. Samiyah watched him intently, and he watched her just as well. She quivered and removed her dress revealing her naked smooth skin underneath. The bikini she wore earlier was never put back on as they rushed to get to the beach house.

Samiyah laid back, slowly spreading her legs allowing Jonas to see everything she was offering. His movements stilled as he watched what he knew would be his dinner on a dish he could never refuse. Her beautiful body put all platters to shame. He removed a condom and tore the paper.

"Let me," she said her voice now sultry and intoxicating.

They switched positions, Jonas now laying on his back.

"Let's play a game," she said.

He raised an inquisitive brow.

"Don't be scared," she teased.

A smirk sat in the corners of his mouth. "What type of game would you like to play, Samiyah?" His voice sent shivers down her bones melting her entirely.

"Put your hands behind your head."

He followed her orders, and she took the condom out but didn't put it on right away. Her hand massaged his length, and he eyed her with a watchful gaze each stroke making him longer and harder than before.

"Don't move," she ordered.

She dipped her head and tasted the beginning of his arousal. A sharp suction left his lips, and he lifted slightly.

"Don't move," she said again, reminding him to stay in formation.

Her tongue teased him with delightful pleasure before taking him in as deep as her throat would open. The taste of his member elevated her greed, and she took in the fullness of him moving in a rhythm that took his breath away. The warmth of her mouth and wetness of her tongue exercised his organ like she was playing an instrument without a second of hesitation.

"Samiyah..." his voice rumbled.

She responded by moving faster; he sat up curtly removing her from the meal she was having. She squealed as the strength in his fingers dug deep into the curves of her waist. He pulled Samiyah on top of him and quickly entered her. A sharp gasp left her mouth at the profound invasion. Her lips trembled slightly as his pelvis met her opening. Still, in an upright position, he slid his hand into her thick tresses and overpoweringly kissed her lips. With her legs folded at his side he moved her back and forth with a forceful thrust that sent moans and songs of praise through each of their mouths.

"Jonas," she said in breathless anticipation.

"Yes, love."

She moaned, their love making temporarily making her lose all thought of her words. He kissed down her neck, pulled back on her hair, indulging on the arch in her neck.

"We..." she paused trying to catch her breath. The more she tried to talk, the deeper he went taking her voice away every time.

"We...what sweetheart," he bit down tenderly on her earlobe. Uncontrollable shivers raced up and down her entire being. Samiyah couldn't formulate an articulate sentence if she wanted to. She was just too far gone to care. Samiyah screamed out, and he went faster lifting her and dropping her to the base of him. He leaned back pulling her with him, her hair hanging to one side.

Samiyah placed her hands on his chest propping herself up, winding her hips in a circular rotation. Suddenly, he flipped her over switching positions with ease. He was in control before, but now he would bear no mercy on her. Jonas dug deep into her womanly core grinding with the force of a drill, his tongue traced her breasts; licking and sucking on her areolas. The sounds of their lovemaking infiltrated the room, and they panted continuing to praise each other. A vibration in her leg gave him a signal that she was close to her end.

"Jonas..." she moaned out.

"I'm with you love." He nibbled on her chin with his hands caressing every part of her.

When her orgasm hit, it was stronger than the night before if that was even possible. Samiyah called out to God and Jonas in intervals of heavy laden breaths. Along with her, Jonas' rush of release coated her insides, without hesitation, he rolled them to the side still connected to her, and they held each other for so long that they fell into a deep slumber.

When Samiyah woke up the next day, she found herself wrapped in a pair of strong arms. Turning to face him was bringing back a strong feeling of sexual awareness. His body did that to her. She could get used to it but she wouldn't. His eyes were still closed, and his face lay within inches of hers with his masculine features softened by his sleep. Although they slept with no blanket, Samiyah found herself warm and cozy. Samiyah continued watching him, thoughts of what could be dancing around in her head.

Even though she knew there wasn't a chance of that happening, she enjoyed wondering anyway. Feeling a spark of confidence, Samiyah turned her lips towards his and placed a soft kiss on his mouth. She kept her eyes on him and before losing her nerve she kissed him again slow and intricate. Samiyah stuck her tongue out and traced the outline of them. Her eyes lowered to his mouth, and she moaned softly, her eyes fluttered back to his to meet a blazing dark gaze. There was a thrill of longing that coursed through her. His lips moved against hers, his arms cuddling her tighter to him. With them still naked, they dived into a morning round of pleasurable sex.

They spent the day together indulging, unable to get enough of each other. For Jonas, he had the strongest ache when it came to her and being there made him put further claims down as they showered, made love, showered again, laughed, talked, ate and made love again. He gave her a tour of the nine bedrooms, five and a half bathroom home. It was a beautiful modern eclectic design that stretched from the soft gray living room walls, blue chairs with burgundy accent pillows, and hardwood floors, to the tan bedroom walls, California King frame, and huge French doors that opened to a balcony with the beach in the backdrop.

For the longest, Samiyah would linger on it looking out at the blue waves. It was such a beautiful sight to behold. They spent breakfast, lunch, dinner, and a little desert there as well. When the sun set, the golden orange glow stretched across the sky giving them a perfect view of a sight that belonged only in fairy tales. Once day turned into night; Jonas and Samiyah watched a romantic comedy that kept them laughing and enjoying the closeness of the other.

For Samiyah she was sinking slowly, and it was beginning to disturb her. Her mind said what Samiyah was feeling was impossible and absurd. Her rational thinking fought a war against another important part of her that had Samiyah believing she was actually feeling a love like she'd never felt before. They fell asleep and when Samiyah awakened, Jonas wasn't in bed. Her movements were slow when she rolled to the side lifting her head slightly. His voice trailed from another room.

"It's no problem at all I should've checked in, my mind has been elsewhere." There was a pause. "Because you know me so well." There was deep laughter. "If you need anything else, let me know."

Silence. A second passed before he was walking back into the room bare-chested with his phone in hand.

"Is everything okay?" Samiyah inquired her voice quiet and dreamy.

He climbed back into bed and pulled her to him, "everything is fine." He kissed her nose. "There's somewhere I want to take you tomorrow with it being our last day here."

She felt a bit apprehensive about that, but she would enjoy every moment with him that she had left.

Chapter Fifteen

On the last day, Jonas drove Samiyah back to the resort so she could prepare herself for whatever adventure he planned next.

"How should I dress," she asked him.

"It's an outdoor activity so dress comfortably."

They kissed and parted ways when the elevator reached her floor. The entire time she'd been there, not one night had been spent in her suite. For a moment, Samiyah thought about spending the rest of her daytime there. Inside she showered and ordered room service while she gathered the clothes she laid out on the bed. She packed them neatly in her suitcase. Realistically, Samiyah needed to get her mind right. This trip was nearly over, and real life was waiting for her in Chicago. But she couldn't shake the feeling of longing that sat deep in her loins. When Samiyah was finished packing, she dressed and blow dried her hair before stepping outside on her balcony.

Her mind traveled to the night they spent in front of his fireplace. In their haste to get to each other, they didn't use a condom. Samiyah tried to inform Jonas of this but once they got started all reasoning flew out the window. She sighed, the last thing she needed was to slip up and get pregnant. Samiyah didn't want to be nobodies baby mama. Minutes later, there was a knock at her door. She glided to the entrance and opened it without asking who was there.

His hands were tucked neatly in his pocket, his muscular build hidden behind a button down casual Perry Ellis shirt with an attractive fit. He kept his eyes on her and stepped in the doorway.

"Are you ready?"

She nodded, her eyes traveled down to his casual shorts that looked comfortable and smooth with a flat front design. Today Jonas had on sandals, and his feet were freshly pedicured.

"If you don't mind, I want to check out first. If we end up staying wherever we're going past check out time, I don't want my belongings to stay behind."

"No one would dare touch your items," he said, forcing her into his hypnotic stare like he always did.

She smiled a bit. "I've already packed everything, and it's ready to go anyway. I'll just grab my suitcase."

"Allow me," he said.

She stepped to the side letting him enter. The nearness of his body awakened hers as if it was trained to rise every time he came around. He must have felt it too because he paused for a short moment before entering the room and grabbing her suitcase. When Jonas exited, the door closed behind him.

"You know that suitcase has wheels. You don't have to carry it," she implied.

He smirked. "I'd rather carry it."

Samiyah loved the deep mellow of his voice, and she was feeling more and more down about their time together ending.

Downstairs at the counter, Samiyah checked out of her suite, and Jonas checked out of the penthouse. When valet brought the Ferrari around, Jonas placed the suitcase in his trunk. As they left the resort, Samiyah sighed dramatically.

"Everything okay," he asked noticing her mood.

She turned slightly to him in her seat. "I want to thank you for this wonderful trip. There is no telling when I would've gotten around to taking a vacation like this."

"Thank you for accepting the invitation." He responded. "We should take more trips like this one."

There it was again; he was talking as if they would always be around each other. "Why do you keep doing that," she asked.

"Doing what?"

"Sometimes you talk as if you plan to marry me." She laughed out loud.

He grinned, enjoying the sound of her voice. "Why is that so funny, Samiyah?"

Her laugh settled down. "Because it's ridiculous."

He switched gears and clenched his jaw never responding to her answer. The mood in the car shifted, and Samiyah cleared her throat.

"This place we're going, is it far?"

"We're almost there actually."

He drove another mile before exiting and pulling into a parking area. They left the vehicle and made their way through a park and down to what looked like a small station. An orange trolley sat unoccupied with a line of people waiting to load.

"Jonas!" A guide walked to him his hand outstretched for a shake.

Jonas smiled and reached forward. "Mark, how are you?"

"I'm doing just fine, it's been a long while, huh?"

Samiyah turned to him. "Everyone keeps saying that."

Jonas chuckled, "Mark this is Samiyah, today is our last day on a short vacation, so I wanted to bring her by and give her a tour."

"Of course, of course," he repeated with a wink at Samiyah.

"Go ahead and find a seat."

Jonas guided Samiyah to the trolley, and they got in.

"I know I've asked about where we're going, but now I'm really curious."

He leaned back and casually placed his arm behind her. "You'll see in no time."

When the trolly finally moved, they traveled down a steep rolling mountainside. Miles of green tropical forest loomed around them. Samiyah relaxed sitting against Jonas as the rich green leaves, shrubbery, and vegetation grew in a display of sublime nature.

When they arrived at their destination and exited the trolley, Jonas slid his hand in hers and led her to the entrance of a massive cave-like structure. Samiyah gasped covering her mouth at the colossal size of it. She was given a pair of headphones.

"What are these for?" she asked.

"It's audio recording. You don't have to wear those; it's just an incentive. This is Cueva Clara it's about one hundred and seventy feet in height."

They made their way through the cave Samiyah in awe at the huge red clay like wall interior with jagged edges hanging from above. About fifteen minutes in Jonas pointed, and Samiyah followed his direction. What looked like a school of bats hung from overhead. She yelped and jumped into his arms. A wide smile covered his handsome face.

His lips touched the edge of her ear. "They won't hurt a soul."

The warmth of his mouth glazed her. They resumed their movements, and she could hear what sounded like water. Samiyah glanced down.

"There's an underground river at a sink hole one hundred and fifty feet deep."

"Will we get to see it," she asked.

He looked at her questionably. "Do you want to?"

After Samiyah thought about it, she decided she didn't want to see it. Jonas laughed, "Don't be scared." He said mocking her from when she told him the same thing a couple of nights before.

The cave walls spread far and deep with different sections breaking off into bottomless crevices of the massive structure.

"This is beautiful. Thank you for bringing me here." Samiyah was so caught up by the breathtaking sight that she didn't notice Jonas was, too. But it had nothing to do with the cave. This he'd seen many times, but Samiyah was becoming his favorite portrait to look at, seeing a different part every time his eyes fell upon her. When their tour ended, Jonas said his goodbyes to the guide, and they headed back to the car.

Samiyah checked the time, it was well into the evening. "I'm going to miss my flight if we don't get to the airport," she said; her mood changing once again to the somberness she held on the way to the caves.

"I would love it if you'd accompany me on my private jet." He paused, "unless you're dying to get away from me." A fleeting smile crossed his face.

A flutter of butterflies flickered in her stomach. "I'd love to."

His attention left the road and traveled to her. For a long moment, they stared at each other. More butterflies fluttered through her. The yearning was so strong, and Samiyah hated it. The last thing she wanted to do was get caught up in a man who could have any woman he wanted. Samiyah kept in mind her reasoning was clear, it made sense, no one could fall for someone this quickly. It was disastrous, and she was playing a dangerous game.

Pulling up to the private strip, Jonas parked the Ferrari mere feet away from the aircraft. They exited, and Jonas removed her suitcase and carried it to the jet. The doors were already extended, and a luxurious pair of steps awaited them. They climbed the stairs and stepped into an all black modern space with leather seats and the initials J. A. R. rooted on the headrests.

"Sit wherever you like." He offered.

Samiyah made herself comfortable in a seat next to the window.

Jonas handed her bag to the stewardess and took a seat next to her. When the jet took off, Samiyah enjoyed the sight below her as she was able to take in the full experience of Puerto Rico from above. Not only was this the most fulfilling, but she would never forget it, and she didn't want to.

Chapter Sixteen

Samiyah's brick one-bedroom townhouse was not a welcomed sight. It represented her failed marriage, and her mind had been clear of David for the last four days. It was blissful really.

"You didn't have to drive me home. I would've been fine in a taxi."

"Don't be ridiculous." Jonas reached out to her and rubbed the tip of her chin. "Let me walk you to your door."

They exited the vehicle. When they approached her door, she faced him. "Thank you again for such a wonderful trip." Her face held a glow from the time they'd spent together.

Jonas reached for Samiyah, his hands gripping her smoothly on her arms. One step, two steps and he had her in his personal space. "I never did get your phone number, Samiyah," he said; his voice low and mellow. "You made me promise we'd always be friends so now it's my duty to make sure we stay in touch."

She exhaled a lite laugh, "You're right." She pulled out her business card and handed it to him. "This one has my cell and office number on it."

His eyes never left hers as his fingers slid up her palm sending shivers through her fingers. He grasped the card. "I won't make you regret it." He grinned.

He kissed her forehead, then lifted her chin with his fingertips for a kiss on her lips. Soft, warm, and mind-boggling was the kiss he laid on her. Samiyah almost whimpered when he pulled back letting her go.

Samiyah opened her door and stepped in closing it behind her. With her mind still with Jonas, she took a look around her entryway. There was no way she could stay here she reasoned. She was moving out.

The next day after spending some time in the local hospital's NICU, Samiyah went about the business of looking for condos around Chicago. Her first visit was to Lake Shore Drive. The petite woman at the counter sprang to her feet as Samiyah entered.

"How are you today? I'm Melissa, are you Samiyah Manhattan?"

Samiyah smiled bright, "Yes I am," she said shaking her hand.

"It's very nice to meet you." The lady said politely. "Tell me a little about what you're looking for, a one bedroom, two, how many adults will occupy the space?"

"Just one adult, that's me. Right now, I'm looking for a studio apartment. I'm moving from a townhome so I can get along fine without the huge size."

Melissa shook her head up and down with a curt smile. "When are you looking to move in?"

"As soon as possible. I know it's last minute."

Melissa waved her off, "Sometimes it just happens that way, no need for an explanation. I've got a studio apartment available to move in next week. We do a criminal background check, a credit check, and reference check. There's also a two hundred dollar application fee. If you're approved, you'll have to pay a fifteen hundred dollar deposit and the first and last months rent. If you've got everything you need today, we can begin the process."

"I did come prepared. However, I would like to see the studio apartment first."

"Of course, follow me."

They strolled through the upscale apartment building and reached the elevators. When the doors opened, they stepped on going up to the third floor.

"The apartment you're showing me, is it a model apartment or is it the one you're looking to lease?"

"It is the one you'll be leasing."

The elevator doors opened, and they strolled to the entrance. Melissa opened it, and they stepped in. The freshly painted space was huge and inviting.

"This is your large living space."

Samiyah took notice of the room. She could fit everything she needed in this area and throw away the rest. The woman walked straight ahead, bearing left.

"This is your kitchen space."

It was a small kitchen with an island separating the areas.

"If we walk across the hallway there's a bathroom and laundry room."

The place was nice and tidy. She decided to go ahead and complete the application process. That process took another hour and a half, as she filled out a form so thick you'd think she was applying to stay at the White House. She shook the lady's hand and said her goodbyes as she made her way through downtown traffic.

Her thoughts turned to Jonas. He didn't call her last night, and she wondered if he had been up all-night thinking about her like she was thinking about him. It was silly, Samiyah kept telling herself. She traveled to River North to the apartment homes EnV. After parking and making her entrance, she met up with another nice lady who showed her around a studio apartment. A recognizable tune resonated in her purse.

"Excuse me for a moment," she dug down in her handbag and lifted it to her ear.

"Samiyah Manhattan." she answered.

"Hey, baby it's your mama."

"Hi mom, how are you?"

"Doing better now that the electrician is here."

"Are you just getting your wiring fixed in the laundry room?"

Her mother sighed, "Yes honey and it's taken all my strength not to lose it on this man."

Samiyah giggled, her mother was a feisty four-foot eleven-inch woman. "What happened, mama?"

"He came up in here, gave it two looks, and now wants to add an additional fee. Then he claimed there was something else that needed to be fixed and wanted to add another fee. I told him straight up if you think for one minute you're getting any extra fee's out of me you're wrong. I'm paying you what you quoted me and nothing more, now fix it before I call Fox news station on you."

Martha Jean was always threatening to call the news station, Better Business Bureau, or the Chicago Tribune on someone's business. It never failed. They always did a lousy job or tried to cheat Martha out of her money, and she would get them right together.

"I'm telling you, they only do it because I'm a woman. Anyway, how you doing, baby?"

"I'm fine mama, currently looking for apartments downtown."

"Oh that's good, you just go right ahead and sell your house and leave that no good scumbag clothes on the side of the road. I knew he was never no good anyway."

Samiyah rolled her eyes. "It's handled, mom. Let me finish up here, and I'll call you back."

"Okay, love you, make sure to call me back."

"I will."

They disconnected the line.

"Sorry about that."

"It's no problem at all.

After taking a look around, Samiyah loved these apartments even more. The floor to ceiling windows gave an open view of Chicago, and she loved the hardwood floors.

"There's a rooftop swimming pool if you'll follow me." And she did. Samiyah had half made up her mind when they exited to the rooftop. Her cell phone rang again. She answered it without checking the caller ID.

"This is Samiyah."

"Good afternoon Samiyah, how are you today?"

Jonas' dark voice sent a tingle through her ear that traveled down her spine. The lady was talking about the amenities while showing Samiyah the large pool area.

"Hello, Jonas, I'm good. How about yourself?"

"Couldn't be better." He paused, "Are you busy?"

"Give me just a moment." She pulled the phone away from her ear and spoke to the nice woman. "I would like to start the application process," she said.

"Great, let's go back down to my office."

Putting the phone back to her ear, she followed her.

"I am in the middle of something. Can I call you back in just a few?"

"I'll make it quick." Jonas said. "I would like to take you out to lunch. Have you eaten today?"

"As a matter of fact, I haven't, and if this application is nearly as long as the last one, then I'll be starving by the time I finish." She laughed softly.

"Application?" he questioned.

"I'm looking for a studio apartment. I'm moving out of the townhouse."

"You didn't waste any time, did you?"

"There is no time like the present."

"You're right about that."

"If you can wait for me, I'll meet up with you for lunch, but if you're hungry now I'll understand."

He chuckled, "Nah, I'm a big boy I want to take you to lunch."

"I promise not to take too long," she said.

"I'll be waiting for your call."

They disconnected the phone.

On the other side, Jonas gazed over the city through his office windows. Last night he'd fallen asleep with Samiyah on his mind. He dreamed of them making love on the beach back in Puerto Rico and having drinks at a theater. This morning, Jonas had gotten an early start running the trail he ran faithfully with Jaden with more thoughts of Samiyah on his mind. Jonas told himself he wouldn't call her today. He'd give her some space to chill out from the vacation. After all, he didn't want to smother her, but Jonas' resistance had weakened and without a second though he called her.

There was a tap at his door. Jonas turned slowly. Amanda, his assistant, lingered in the doorway.

"Come in Amanda, have a seat," he said.

She walked into the room and sat in his chair. Today she'd built up the guts to tell him how she felt, but now sitting in front of his six-foot four-inch frame, looking back at his intimidating stare, she was losing her nerve.

"What can I do for you," he asked, moving to his desk reclaiming his chair.

Amanda decided to play it safe, "There's an event coming up that I've volunteered for and I was hoping maybe you could help me out if it is at all possible. You know I wouldn't usually ask you for anything," she blushed and befuddled, "only if it suits you, of course."

"You mean there's finally something I can do for you?" He winked and smiled softly. "Whatever it is, I would love to help. Give me the details."

Amanda lit up. "There's an auction benefit for the March of Dimes gala in three weeks. I know usually you attend these events so I was wondering if you could place a bid on me." She smiled shyly. "I'd hate for one of those rich old men to get the date then I'd spend most of my night fighting off their advances. We don't actually have to go on a date or anything," she continued to fumble.

Jonas chuckled, "Oh come on now they can't be that bad."

A look of horror displayed across her face. Jonas laughed even harder, "I'm just joking. Of course, I'll bid on you, and I'd love to show you to a nice evening."

"Oh thank you so much. You don't know how much this means to me." She stood from her chair, and so did he. Amanda rounded his desk but once near him she took tentative steps closer. When she was so close she could smell his cologne, Amanda reached out and hugged him. He charmingly hugged her back.

"You're the best," she said before leaving his office.

The office phone shrilled. It came straight through to his extension, "Jonas Alexander Rose," he answered.

"How was your vacation, son?"

"Hey pop, it was by far the best one I've had all year."

"That's good. It wouldn't have anything to do with your lady friend would it?"

Jonas smirked, his father was always trying to figure out if he'd finally found the woman that would bare his grandchildren. "What lady friend?"

His father huffed, "Stop yanking my chain. You know good and well who I'm referring too."

"Whenever I get serious with someone trust me, dad, you'll be the first to know."

"What did I tell you about when a man says trust me?"

"It means he can't be trusted." They chorused.

"That rule doesn't apply to me, pop. You know you can trust me."

"I swear if I leave it up to you boys I'll never get any grandchildren."

"Don't even think about it. The last time you tried to hook me up I had to fight off the woman's mother."

Christopher burst into laughter. "I'm glad you find that so amusing," Jonas said.

"Oh shush son, that was one time."

"The time before that I had to fend off a friend, and before that a sibling. I don't know where you're getting these women, but just leave it to me. I'm my own man; I can find my own woman when I'm ready," Jonas said.

"And just when will you be ready?"

"When I can find a love like you had with mom." His father had become silent now. Jonas thought back to the memories of his childhood. "You moved in sync like you were one. You would come home from work and even after a long day of working herself she would still greet you at the door. You were everything to her. On weekends, I would catch you staring at her while she cleaned up around you, then out of the blue, you'd grab her hand and I remember you saying Mrs. Rose, you're like a flower that continues to bloom. Her face would light up, you guys would kiss, and I would yell gross," he chuckled.

"And that's how we would catch you every time."

"You and mom set impossible standards. The woman that has my children would have to come close at least."

"From father to son, when you meet the woman that dominates your thoughts, who's noble, trustworthy, and strong-minded, you should snatch her up. Nowadays they're not many like that."

"Hence the reason why I tell you to let me handle this on my own. No more butting in."

"If you promise me one thing."

Jonas was almost afraid to ask. "What's that pop?"

"Don't tell your brothers I let you off the leash because I plan to still bug them about finding a woman."

They laughed.

"Yes, sir."

"I'll let you go for now."

"The next time I take a trip to Puerto Rico, I want you with me. No excuses."

His father was quiet again; Jonas knew how his father felt about the island. It held just as many memories as the home he lived in.

"I can't make you any promises."

"Pop."

"Call me later, son." The line went dead. Jonas placed the phone in its cradle and sat back, his chair dipping, swaying to the side. He folded his hands behind his head and thought about their conversation. There was already a woman dominating his thoughts, and he couldn't help but wonder if he dominated hers.

Chapter Seventeen

Much to Samiyah's dismay, the application process had taken just as much time if not more to fill out. It seemed that the upscale rental properties were rigorous with future tenants. She made her way into the restaurant and searched for Jonas. When her eyes landed on him, he was sitting at a booth nursing what looked to be a glass of water with lemon. She approached him, putting an extra sway in her steps. He leaned back comfortably and met her watchful stare. A delightful smile swept across his handsome face, and he stood as she pulled up in front of him.

"Hello beautiful," he said pulling her in for a hug.

"Hello to you, too. Have you not had enough of me yet?" she joked.

"Nah, I'm still getting my fill of you."

She laughed softly, "Is that so?"

He loved the way she laughed, so sexy, soft and pleasant.

"That is so."

They pulled apart and sat across from each other getting relaxed and ordered their food.

"So apartment hunting, huh?"

"Yes, it's time for me to move forward."

"Is that truly what you want to do?"

"Definitely."

"That bad, huh?"

"Well, you were there to experience a small percentage of what our relationship has been like for the last couple of years. After finding out he'd been with his mistress for most of our marriage, I honestly was ready to sign the papers immediately. But after giving it some thought, I did want to try counseling."

"But he didn't?"

Samiyah swallowed, her eyebrows furrowed. "No." She glanced out the window.

"Samiyah, God works in mysterious ways. When one door closes another one opens, and you better believe it opens for the better."

Bringing her eyes back to his, Samiyah pondered on Jonas' words as his piercing stare tore through her. The waiter appeared with their food.

"Tell me something about you I don't know, Jonas."

He smiled, "Hmmm what is interesting about Jonas Alexander Rose."

"A lot I'm sure," Samiyah responded.

Jonas' smile grew showing his pearly white teeth. "On Tuesdays and Thursday, I visit the Boys and Girls Clubs and mentor the young men there. The organizer tells me they're a handful, but I've yet to see it."

"Maybe they're on their best behavior when you're around."

"You might be right."

"How many boys is it that you mentor?"

"It's a full class. Whoever is in attendance."

"That's very nice."

"These young men need someone to teach them the ropes. Show them how to make their dreams a reality."

"Who better than someone who's worked hard, stayed out of trouble and built his own wealth?" Samiyah sang.

"That person sounds perfect. Next time you speak to him, ask if he could mentor me," Jonas teased.

They laughed and ate casually; their conversation going from sports to the presidential debates. When their conversation switched to Jonas' parents, he didn't seem as forthcoming as before. Jonas glanced at the time on his watch.

"Do you need to get back to the office? I know I've held up enough of your time today," Samiyah said.

"This time was well spent, I'd love to do it again." His dreamy voice cruised across the table settling over her. Samiyah blushed.

"So would I."

An unbearably gorgeous grin spread across his face. "Let me walk you to your car."

He asked for the check and left a tip. They exited the restaurant making it to her car quicker than she liked.

"So friend, when will I see you again," she said turning full circle to look at him.

"Anytime, you name it." He closed the gap and lay a kiss on her cheek.

The warmth from his kiss turned her into mush. Samiyah inhaled deeply. "You have to stop kissing me like that."

"Why is that?"

"Because I might get carried away and start to get the impression that we're more than friends. And well, you know how straightforward you are. A fling's a fling, right?"

Jonas pulled back slightly making eye contact with her.

"If I am to be honest with you, Samiyah, I would say this thing between us surpassed friendship and was never as simple as a mere fling."

Her insides melted and Samiyah tried to reason with the rational side of her brain. Unfortunately, his closeness left her incapable of thinking clearly.

"While I do feel," Samiyah hesitated to look for the right word, "strongly about our chemistry, I'm not sure if now's the right time for whatever this thing is." She admitted.

"I disagree."

Jonas bent down and kissed her lips, his hands slipping into her hair with a firm grip. With an intense pull, her lips parted slightly, and she moaned into his mouth. With his other arm wrapping around her,

Samiyah floated into a cloud of ecstasy. With each tug of her lips, she was falling further away from her rationale. A car pulled into a parking space next to them, and the passengers got out and walked away. The alarm chirped bringing Samiyah back from the depths of passion. She pulled away from him breaking their kiss stepping to the side.

"I have to go."

She said quickly making a hasty retreat. Jonas didn't stop her. He stepped back and watched her run for dear life, but it didn't matter, Samiyah wouldn't get far. Jonas had made up his mind, that she was the one he wanted.

"So, how was the trip and I want details," Claudia said.

Samiyah made it back to her townhome when she got the call from her best friend and business partner. She grabbed a basket of clothes and went into the laundry room.

"It was heavenly," she breathed with a sigh.

Claudia squealed, "Ooooh, I am not jealous, I am not jealous," she chanted trying to convince herself.

Samiyah laughed. "You should be," she teased.

"Okay, I am jealous." The women fell out laughing.

"Girl, what happened?"

"You mean besides the fact that I was basically joined at the hip with Mr. Smooth Operator the entire time?"

"Oh don't act like you didn't like it!"

"Quite the opposite, I loved it." Samiyah sighed again.

"Then why do you sound so sad about it? Perk up. You had one of the finest men in Chicago at your beck and call. There is nothing to be down about."

"I'm not down, I'm just confused and a little unsettled."

"About what?"

"He took me out to lunch today, I've not too long ago returned, and he makes it seem as if he wants to date me. At first, I thought I was just looking too deep into his comments, but he confirmed today that he wants to be more than friends."

Claudia switched the phone from one ear to the other. "I'm still waiting on the part that's confusing and unsettling," she spoke evenly.

"How about the part where I just divorced my husband not too long ago."

"So because you're newly divorced, that's good enough reason to not fall in love with Mr. Right?"

Samiyah huffed, Claudia was not making this easy for her. "As a matter of fact, it is! And how would you know he's Mr. Right? We all know the reputation of men of his stature."

"Okay, but how does he treat you when you're together? Do you feel like arm candy, bedroom candy, or what?"

Samiyah didn't have to think about it long. "No, no, none of that. He's a perfect gentleman." Her voice dipped low, soft and easy. "He gives me his undivided attention, we've talked about a little bit of everything. For God's sake, I even cried on his shoulder about my father while we were walking down the beach." She smiled at the remembrance.

"Then don't you think you should give him a chance?" Claudia said. "Don't cheat yourself, treat yourself."

Samiyah knew Claudia was right, but she was genuinely afraid to take it there. "I don't know."

Samiyah added detergent to her washing machine, turned her back and leaned against it for support.

"Seriously Samiyah, what do you have to lose?"

"I don't know, but hey let me call you back, I told my mother I would return her call, and if I don't she'll swear I'm neglecting her."

Claudia laughed, "Tell Ms. Jean I said hi."

"Okay." They hung up, and Samiyah dialed her mother.

"I was wondering if you were going to call me back. If I were dead and gone, you'd wish I was here." Samiyah rolled her eyes.

"Mama please don't start that."

"I'm just saying."

"Did you get the wires in your laundry room fixed, and Claudia says hi."

"Yes, and I kicked him right out with a check for the amount he quoted. Tell Claudia I said hello. But that's not what I called you earlier to talk to you about. Who's this guy you're on the front of the newspaper with? I don't have to tell you that men ain't no good and all they want is what's in between your legs. Especially men like this handsome young fella on here. Looks can be deceiving child and all that glitters ain't gold."

Samiyah's head fell back, and she closed her eyes feeling a headache coming on.

"If you're just having fun, that's fine but don't give any more time than that. I don't want to see you hurt again, baby."

More silence from Samiyah. "Well say something. Don't get quiet, you know I'm telling the truth."

"Mom please."

"Please what?"

"He's just a friend."

"Un huh, don't you lie to me. This gorgeous man right here ain't no woman's friend."

"Mom, I've got to go I'm washing clothes."

"If you want to rush me off the phone, that's fine by me, but you know I'm right."

"I love you mom, bye."

Samiyah disconnected the call and redialed Claudia.

"That was quick."

"Girl I love my mama, but sometimes she can be such a prude."

"What she say?"

"She saw us on the front of the Chicago Tribune."

"Oh my goodness." Claudia said, "Listen, I know how Mama Jean is but let me tell you, don't you listen to her. You know she thinks all men are evil."

"Yeah, but she was right about my ex."

"And what do Jonas and your ex have in common?"

Samiyah didn't need to think about it. "Nothing."

"Exactly."

Chapter Eighteen

Jonas usually spent his time driving through rush hour traffic with jazz music bellowing from his speakers. It was a good way to keep his mind clear of the bumper to bumper road rage that went on around him. But today as he made his way to the Boys and Girls Club, nothing could clear his mind from thoughts of Samiyah. She'd taken off running like something was after her yesterday evening, and Jonas couldn't blame her. He understood her need to get away more than she thought which is why he didn't stop her.

Deep down inside, Jonas was fighting his own battle. Never in a million years had he found himself this taken by a woman. The fact that it happened so quickly was all the more stunning to him. But he'd made up his mind that he wouldn't let her get away, he couldn't. If he did, he'd live the rest of his life wondering what could've been and Jonas was not a man who liked to live with regrets. He'd had the dissatisfaction of living with only a few of those, and he would do whatever was necessary to make sure he didn't add more regrets to the pile.

He grabbed his cell phone and dialed her number but didn't hit send. Maybe she needed a little space he reasoned. He removed the number and placed his phone back in the middle console. He would leave her be for now, but tomorrow he would make it his business to reach out to her.

He pulled into the facility and parked. As he made his way into the building, a young boy ran up to him.

"Mr. Rose!"

He gave the boy a bright smile and pat on the head. "Hey David, I'm glad you're here today. How's school?"

The six-grader shrugged his shoulders, "It's alright I guess."

"You guess, what seems to be the problem?"

"It's a new school; I don't know anybody there. All my friends went to different schools or are still back at my old school."

"That's because you graduated. It's a stepping stone. That's a good thing. I'm sure your parents are proud of you."

"Yeah, my mom says this is the best school for my academics. Whatever that means."

Jonas chuckled, "I'm sure your mom is right."

"She says, she's always right," David said.

Jonas laughed again, "Sure she is. Come on let's go inside."

They walked into the building and John Ripley, the organizer there, walked out of his office to shake his hand.

"Mr. Rose, how are you today, son?"

"I can't complain, how about yourself?"

"I wouldn't dare complain. The wife may overhear me and have my head on a platter."

The men chuckled.

"David, what are you doing out of the classroom?"

"I saw Mr. Rose pull up and wanted to say hi."

"You could've done that when he got in the building."

"It's no problem at all," Jonas responded.

"Run along now, son, Mr. Rose will be there in just a minute."

David left for the classroom.

"I wanted to ask you; we've just put up an open spot for a female mentor to come in and replace Sandra. If you know of anyone, pass along the information, please." He handed Jonas a folder.

"What happened to Sandra?"

"Apparently, she got an internship in Ohio that she couldn't refuse, so her last day here was last week."

"Good for her," Jonas said.

"But not so good for us." Mr. Ripley countered.

"I'm sure you'll find someone just a great as Sandra to replace her."

"Maybe, but that could take more time than we have. Those girls don't need to go too long without a mentor."

Jonas thought about Samiyah. "I may have someone I can ask."

"Perfect, I can always count on you! Now I'll let you get to your class."

Jonas entered the classroom, and the loud talking died down. He placed the folder on his desk and made his way to the front of it perching his hip on the edge. He had them write out a list of goals they wanted to achieve.

Some of them being younger than others had fairly comical responses as other had real goals in mind.

"I want to know how I can get a car like the one you have sitting outside Mr. Rose," said an eighth grader sitting in the back.

"I want you to tell me," Jonas said. The young boy thought for a minute.

"I need a job?" It was more of a question.

"What kind of job do you need?"

"One that makes a lotta money." The boys laughed.

Jonas smiled, "And how do you find a job that pays a lotta money as you put it?"

"One that I build for myself."

"What kind of job do we call that?"

"Self-employment."

"So, tell me Matthew, what steps do you need to take to be self-employed to make a lot of money?"

"First, I need to set a goal, then I need to write out a plan to meet that goal. I have to work hard, save, and look for sponsors."

"And what else?"

The boy continued to answer Jonas as he continued to fire question after question at him. It was no doubt that Jonas was impressed and proud that the kids were paying attention, especially since he wasn't able to mentor them every day. Jonas randomly called on other boys in the room to make sure they were all paying attention.

Surely enough they all made valid points and gave some insight on how they would attain their goals. After forty-five minutes of the back and forth answer session, Jonas decided to break so the boys could grab snacks and sodas provided by the organization. There was a lite tap at the door.

"The door is open." He spoke loudly.

When it swung open Samiyah timidly stood in the doorway. Jonas felt a plethora of emotions seeing her statuesque form standing before him.

"I hope I'm not interrupting, but when you get a moment, there is pizza in the cafeteria for the boys." A dazzling smile crossed her face. "Don't wait too long though; the girls already beat you guys to it." She said demurely.

The boys turned to Jonas eyes wide already standing to their feet. "Go ahead fellas."

They flew out of the room, with Samiyah standing to the side so she wouldn't be trampled. As the last boy left the room, Jonas walked toward her.

"Pizza?"

"I figured you guys could use something to eat. Are you hungry?"

His eyes faltered as he reached her. "I'm always hungry."

Her body lit up with a slow burn that made her squirm.

"I hope you don't mind me barging in."

"I don't mind at all. It is a welcomed interruption."

A smile lingered on his lips. He had a way of standing right up on her that made his presence and invasion of privacy. However, Samiyah couldn't find it in herself to step away. Jonas had this paralyzing aura that held her feet firmly in place. She couldn't deny that this man hypnotized her in a way no one had ever done. And for the brief time they'd been away from each other, she'd missed him.

After talking to Claudia, the day before, Samiyah decided to let her guard down, no matter how much the practical side of her tried to talk her out of it.

She leaned in slipping a quick kiss on his lips before moving off toward the cafeteria. He reached out pulling her back in. His lips hovering over hers.

"Jonas... we're in public. Around kids."

That seemed to do it. Instantly Jonas released Samiyah and took a step back. "It might have saved you this time, but it won't save you later." He warned.

She batted her eyes, "I'm counting on it."

She turned and sashayed away; his eyes glued to her. When he blinked and looked off, the organizer, Mr. Ripley stood watching them from his office a huge grin displayed on his face. He winked and gave Jonas a thumbs up. Jonas chuckled and made his way to the cafeteria.

Later that night, Samiyah found herself wrapped tightly with Jonas, their bodies merging into one erotic display of passion. With their moans and whispers of love, they sang out to one another with orgasmic eruptions taking them higher than anything either of them had ever experienced before. Nights turned into days and days into nights as they reveled in each other, growing a love that neither of them thought was possible.

Samiyah took on a part time mentorship over the young girls at the club until they could find someone full time. But the girls fell in love with her wittiness and sense of humor.

They soaked up every word she dished out like a sponge, and before long, the organizer asked her to step in for a full-time role. Unfortunately, that would interfere with her time with the preemies. As much as she wanted to help, Samiyah denied the role for obvious reasons.

"I understand," the organizer said. "But the girls might not." He tried to tug on her heart strings.

"They'll never miss what they didn't have. Part time is what they're used to so let's not tell them you asked." She patted him on the shoulder. "I've got some packing to do so I should go, but I'm sure you'll find someone equally as fantastic as me." She smiled brightly, dipped into a curtsey and left.

Chapter Nineteen

Samiyah lifted a cardboard box and placed it on top of another that sat in the corner of her bedroom. She'd been approved for the luxury apartment at EnV, so she busied herself packing. She wasn't officially moving in for another two weeks, but this would put her ahead. Her mother had instilled in her at a very young age about taking care of her responsibilities.

That included bills, children if she ever saw fit to have any, and anything else she signed her name on. Samiyah had done just that. As of right now her box spring and mattress was standing on edge against the wall, her frame unscrewed and taken down. That box was the last of the things she needed to pack in regard to her bedroom, and she was officially moving downstairs to her living room. Samiyah's life had taken a turn. Gone were the days of mourning her marriage to David. Her future was looking brighter by the day, and she was excited about moving into her new place.

Her phone lit up setting off a notification. She retrieved it and looked at the screen. It was a reminder that the March of Dimes benefit auction was in three weeks. She'd been thinking about it off and on. The closer the day came the more nervous she became. Since she and Jonas had been spending time together practically every day, she wondered if she should tell him about it. It was no secret really. All of Chicago's elite would be in attendance. It wouldn't surprise her if Jonas were going. However, he hadn't mentioned it.

Well, you haven't either.

Her eyes scanned the time on her device, and she decided to take him dinner. The last time she'd spoken to him, he was still at his office. He worked diligently trying to get another Rose Bank and Trust Credit Union branch opened in New Jersey. She made her way to the bathroom.

The head scarf she wore was doing nothing for her appearance. She removed it and changed her shirt into a light-colored blouse. She decided to leave on her blue jeans and wrap her hair up into a tight ponytail leaving her neck on full display. She applied some lip gloss to shine up her full lips and added small diamond studs in her ear. Samiyah tried to pull off the most casual look but was failing miserably. She checked her teeth and opened her mouth sticking her tongue out. With one hand cupped to her mouth, she smelled her breath. Satisfied at the outcome, Samiyah left the townhouse and stopped by a Chinese restaurant. After picking up their order, she made her way to Jonas' building.

It wasn't too difficult to find a parking spot since most people had already left for the day. She cut her engine and made her way to the entrance.

At the sudden knock on the door, Jonas looked up from his MAC book pro laptop. A small smile lit up his lips, and he sat back in his swivel chair placing his hands behind his head.

"You're still here," he said. "I thought you were gone for the day."

Amanda stepped into the room with a bag in her hand. "I did leave, but since you hadn't called and asked me to go save the wildlife animals, I thought I'd come by and check on you." She gave a light-hearted laugh.

His smile stretched further across his face. "Is that your way of telling me I work you too hard?"

"Yes, but it's okay I can handle it." Her eyes faltered. Amanda was feeling herself tonight. Truth be told she'd went to the restaurant downstairs and had a few Corona's. The alcoholic beverage had given her the courage she needed to come back and approach Jonas the way she'd always wanted to.

Her eyes lingered on his handsome face, giving him direct eye contact. She wanted him to feel where she was coming from before she spoke again. He dropped his focus to the bag in her hand.

"What do you have there?"

"I picked up something from the restaurant downstairs, and I'm sure you haven't eaten. Tell me I'm wrong?"

"So, you think you know me now?" he joked; his smooth voice sending tingles through her. She moved closer to him and rounded his desk coming up inches away from him. She dangled the plastic bag with the styrofoam container in front of him.

He put his nose close to the bag and moaned softly. "Mmmm, that smells good. Thank you very much." He reached for the bag, and their fingers touched. On instinct, Amanda enclosed her fingers around his.

"My, my, Mr. Rose your hands are rugged yet soft at the same time. How is that possible?" she gave his hand a gentle squeeze.

"Are you trying to feel me up, Amanda?" He joked again.

She shrugged, "Maybe?" her voice low and flirty now.

He chuckled and removed his hand as politely as possible. Amanda took another step towards him but miscalculated her movement and fell over into his lap.

"Oh!" she yelped.

Quickly, Jonas moved his hands to catch her, wrapping one sturdy arm around her waist while the other held on to the bag containing the food.

"Careful," he said, "you don't want to hurt yourself."

Amanda pulled back to look at him.

"Sorry, I must have had one too many Corona's."

"I'd say so."

"Hey, I wanted to thank you again in advance for bidding on me tomorrow night. I appreciate you."

"I'm sure you'll be the most beautiful woman in the house, so I'll consider myself lucky to have a date with you." He gave a genuine smile.

Noticing a hint of a shadow, Jonas leaned away from her towards the door. "Samiyah." He said surprised at her arrival. He stood to his feet, while simultaneously helping Amanda to hers. Amanda turned around equally surprised but annoyed by her visit.

"Hello Jonas," her eyes went from him to Amanda then back to him. "I stopped by to bring you dinner." She walked into the room and dropped the Chinese bag on his desk. "But it looks like you already have some. My apologies for interrupting." She turned and beat a hasty departure.

"Samiyah!" he yelled rounding his desk to chase her down.

Samiyah kept moving. She'd been standing at the door long enough to catch their flirty vibes. Seeing Amanda's hand in his put her on edge, but seeing Amanda in his lap was enough. What could his excuse possibly be? At least she knew now that Jonas would be at the benefit and he already had a date picked out. She felt like such a sore loser. Samiyah had gone years ignoring the signs that her ex-husband was being dishonest and she wouldn't do it again.

"Samiyah!" Jonas shouted getting to her before she could enter the elevator. He grabbed her arm, and she spun around a glare in her eyes.

"Don't!" she said.

"Baby, it's not what you think."

She tisked, "Could've fooled me. Look it's my fault, I knew what kind of man you were before I let my guard down. It's okay." She tried to wiggle out of his grasp, but he held firm.

"Please let me explain, I know how it looked, but it was really innocent. I had no idea Amanda was bringing me dinner. I had no idea you were either, and you're not the only one who let their guard down. I have too, more than you realize." He pleaded with his eyes for her to understand.

"You," she pointed sticking her finger in his chest, "let your guard down? Tell me, Jonas, how did you do that when every time the subject of your parents come up you become instantly mute. Or when the topic of your retirement comes up, something that should be easily explained but again you become silent. You're not really letting me in Jonas. It's like you've built a fortress and it's completely impenetrable."

He sighed, "It's not that I don't want to share it with you. It's just, just..."

"Just what? I'm really intrigued to know. Why did you hang up your boxing gloves, Jonas? You're young, still in your prime, and undefeated. So tell me why'd you do it?"

He hesitated a minute too long. Samiyah shook her head in dismay. "That's what I thought." She freed herself and stepped onto the elevator. They eyed each other in the most intense showdown as the doors closed taking Samiyah to her car.

Later that night Samiyah found herself staring at the ceiling fan as she lay on the sofa in her living room. Her mind roamed with thoughts of what she'd witnessed at Jonas' office. Since she'd left, he'd called her several times, and she'd wanted to answer on more than one occasion. However, the smart side of her was holding firm.

Over and over again she'd told herself now was not the right time to get involved with anyone, but her heart had told another story. Now she felt even worse than she did before. She sighed and closed her eyes trying to shut out the unwanted thoughts. Her phone rang, and she didn't bother looking at it. If she did, she might just answer it.

Chapter Twenty

"Why didn't you just hire a moving company to come over here and get all this stuff?" Martha Jean dropped a box inside the U-Haul with a heavy thud.

"Mom, I told you I would move heavy boxes you just get the light stuff."

"There ain't no more light stuff, and I don't wanna be standing around watching you and Claudia do everything when I'm here. I might as well help."

Samiyah sighed and wiped her forehead with the back of her hand. "Why don't you just have a seat on the passenger side until we finish. There's not much left."

"You didn't answer my question. Why didn't you hire a moving company?"

"Because I can do it myself."

"But you're not doing it yourself, are you?"

Samiyah loved her mother, but she was really working her nerves right now. "I know you at least know a few men who could've helped us."

"What you like for me to call David?"

Martha Jean turned her nose up. "Now you tryna be funny?"

"That's the only man I know!"

"What about that guy you were all cuddled up on the newspaper with, he looked strong enough to carry this whole house on his back."

With the conversation switched to Jonas, Claudia interjected her two sense, "Oh yeah what about him Samiyah, you know he's got six brothers. I'm sure, if you would've asked they wouldn't mind helping."

"Six brothers!" Martha Jean screeched.

Samiyah stacked a cardboard box on top of the one her mother placed in the truck. "Seriously? Now you want me to call him? I thought all men were evil and they only wanted one thing, mama. Make up your mind!"

"Well I didn't say go and fall in love with him. But six brothers? You should've asked. That's just common sense."

Samiyah rolled her eyes. She felt like a teenager being chastised. "If you must know, I don't talk to him anymore. You should be proud mama, mission accomplished."

"Excuse me, what mission would that be?"

"The mission to make sure I'm just as single and alone as you for the rest of my life!"

Martha Jean opened her mouth to respond but closed it. "Ladies, let's not get out of hand, okay?" Claudia turned to Samiyah; her face frowning into a worried countenance.

"I'm only trying to help you. All men cheat, they're all liars, what is wrong with me wanting to save you a lifetime of heartache?"

"Forget about it," Samiyah waved her hand dismissing the conversation.

"No, I can't forget about it now. You brought it up, it must be something you've held in for a long time now but let me tell you; I am not lonely! I am fine just the way I am. And I'd rather be by myself then put my trust in another rusty, dusty, man!"

"Well that's you! I don't want to be alone for the rest of my life, and there's nothing wrong with that! If I have to go through a few heartaches just to meet the man I'll spend the rest of my life with then so be it! But it would help mom if you could provide some understanding and support my decision to have one. Sure, I know your marriage failed, my marriage failed but newsflash it's not the end of the world!"

Samiyah turned and went inside the house dragging the dolly behind her. Martha and Claudia followed closely. "You know what, fine! From now on you won't hear me say anything about your life!"

"Thank you very much." Samiyah was exhausted. Not from moving but the back and forth between her and her mom. It had been nine years since her father and mother divorced and ever since all she'd heard was her mother's venom when it came to men. Martha went and stood against a wall with her arms folded looking like a child in time out.

She watched Samiyah and Claudia, as they moved the washing machine onto the dolly and took it to the truck. When they came back for the dryer, she was still perched up mumbling something incoherent to herself. She cut her eyes at Samiyah as she walked past then left the room to go outside for a smoke.

It had been five years since Martha had a cigarette. No doubt the end of her marriage caused her to start. However, Martha called it quits after figuring out how much money she spent on smoking per year; an overwhelming figure that knocked some sense into her real quick. Martha pulled out her electronic cigarette and leaned against the van, continuing to mumble underneath her breath. A luxury four-door sedan pulled in front of the mailbox and parked.

Martha Jean blew out a cloud of smoke peering at the expensive vehicle. Jonas stepped out in a casual gray V-neck t-shirt and jeans that hung slightly off of his hips. He slipped off the ultra-violet sunglasses that adorned his face as he jumped the curb to approach her.

"Good afternoon."

Martha's eyebrows arched no doubt noticing how handsome Jonas was up close. The newspaper did him no justice. "She's inside." Was her bland statement.

"Am I interrupting?"

"If you're going to help us pack up this truck then no, if not then yes."

He chuckled, "I'm Jonas Alexander Rose," he reached for a handshake. Martha tilted her head to the side and blew out smoke. "Are you here to help or not?"

"As long as you need me."

"That's more like it," she said accepting his handshake. "Come inside," she put her vaporizer away and walked to the house. When they stepped in, Samiyah came face to face with him. She paused, "What are you doing here?"

"I'm here to help wherever you need me." His gaze bore into her making her insides melt.

Keep your focus, Samiyah reprimanded herself. "Thank you, but we don't need your help."

"Jonas don't you listen to a word my daughter is saying. She has a bad attitude today. Don't pay her no mind." Martha grabbed Jonas arm, "Follow me."

They went upstairs. Samiyah rubbed the temples of her head. "Girl are you really going to let that man get away," Claudia whispered.

Samiyah gave her a warning look, picked up another box and headed to the U-Haul with Claudia on her heels. She put the box down and turned to her, "Don't start okay. I just want to get this done and over with."

Claudia put her hands on her hips. "You know, you're not fooling anyone. I know you still want that man and your mother does, too."

"Okay, you got me, but it doesn't mean a thing. Now move out of my way."

They exited the truck just as Jonas came downstairs carrying the queen size box spring. "Excuse me ladies." He winked at Samiyah, and she couldn't help but watch as he walked to the truck.

"Your mouth is hanging open," Claudia whispered in her ear. Samiyah swatted her. "Shut up!"

Claudia yelped and ran to the kitchen to get another box. On his way back in, Jonas stopped in front of her. "Can we talk."

"I don't have time, as you can see I'm busy." She turned to leave, and he reached out for her halting her departure. She side eyed him.

"Please, I haven't heard from you in two weeks."

"After you take this mattress to the truck. Oh, and these dressers, and this TV," Martha imposed.

Jonas flashed her a heartwarming smile. "Of course," he said.

Samiyah peered at her mom but didn't say anything. She didn't want to argue with her any more than she had to.

"Well, at least he's good for more than that so-called husband of yours! He wouldn't lift a finger. I hate lazy men."

"You hate all men mama!"

"Well," she stuck her lip out watching Jonas. "Maybe not."

"I can't even..."

"You can't even what?" Martha folded her arms.

"Nothing," Samiyah went to the kitchen to find Claudia. She found her talking in hush tones on her cell phone.

"I gotta go, I'll speak with you later." She ended the call.

"Don't try and get out of helping me. You're mine all day."

"Girl you don't need me, you've got that sexy Casanova doing it all for you."

Samiyah rolled her eyes. "That is all my mother's doing, it has nothing to do with me."

Claudia twisted her lips. "Who are you trying to convince, me or yourself?"

"Can you just help me get this chair into the truck?"

Claudia pointed towards the living room. Jonas was lifting the furniture with ease, carrying more than one piece at a time. "Like I said, you don't need me and I ain't mad about it."

Samiyah felt warm and fuzzy all over. Jonas crossed her mind on a daily basis. He'd gotten into her soul in a way that was a bit frightening. But she wouldn't let him win. She couldn't, no good men seemed to be attracted to her, and she had to break those chains. She turned back to Claudia. "I don't understand my mother. One minute she's fussing about trying to save me from heartbreak. The next she seems to be purposely keeping him around."

"Well you did ask her to show some understanding and you made it loud and clear that you didn't want to be alone. So maybe she's trying to do that."

"I didn't expect her to do a complete turnaround asap!"

"Hold your horses; this is your mama we're talking about. That still doesn't mean she couldn't possibly be trying. You are her only child. She loves you." They watched as Martha pointed from one thing to the next. Jonas never wavering in assisting with the heavy lifting.

"He's actually a good packer," Claudia said. He'd moved around some of the boxes and situated furniture in an order that would get everything in the truck to make one trip.

"And we couldn't possibly move that fast. His adrenaline is astonishing. Must be nice," Claudia cooed.

A shudder crawled through Samiyah's bones. The thought of his adrenaline transporting her back to their many sex sessions in Puerto Rico. Claudia glanced at her watch. "I don't want to interrupt what I know is some steamy thoughts, but If we want to get this done before it gets dark, we better get going."

Samiyah blinked several times trying to get her mind right, but every time he moved she would drown in the brief sight of his abs, the flex of his arms, and the grin he would give her mother after she'd boss him around to do something else.

With the living room now bare, her feet finally moved, and she lifted the last of the boxes in the kitchen. Like a zombie, Samiyah stepped out the front door; her mind still reeling with thoughts of him. He went to her taking the box out of her arms.

"That goes in the car," she said. "Thank you for helping, you didn't have to."

"I wanted to." He closed the car door. "Can we talk now."

"There's nothing to say."

"Why are you running from me?"

"I'm not running. I'm being smart. I don't need a man nor should I be pretending I want one."

A look of surprise crossed his face. "Pretending?"

Samiyah had no idea why she'd said that, but since she did, she stuck with it. "Yes, pretending."

"So, you're saying the connection we have is all in my head?"

"You were nice; we had a good time in Puerto Rico. I appreciated the trip. That's it. We're back in the real world, now, let's not twist reality. I don't need you to help me unpack this stuff since the condo I'm moving to has a moving staff. It was nice knowing you." She held her hand out.

Jonas was not one for begging or trying to convince anyone, but he couldn't bring himself to walk away from her.

"Liar," he said.

"Excuse me?"

"You heard me; the reality is you're running scared. You think because you've had a bad relationship that somehow all men will turn out to disappoint you. And you're wrong."

Samiyah bit her bottom lip. "Are you going to prove me wrong, the man I saw flirting with his assistant? I can't compete with her. She's around you for everything, knows your every move, and frankly, I don't want to. Do whatever you like."

She tried to side-step him, but he blocked her exit. "I wasn't flirting with her."

Samiyah glared at him.

"I know what it looked like, but it was really platonic. I'm sure she's grown to have a love for me, and I do her, but it's not in the way that you think," Jonas said.

"If you really believe that, then you are blind and I won't be a part of whatever it is she thinks you have going on." She pushed through him.

"Samiyah!"

Samiyah jumped in the driver's seat of the U-Haul and pulled off with her mother following closely in tow.

"Are you okay?" Claudia asked.

Samiyah didn't know, but one thing was for certain, she was definitely running.

Chapter Twenty One

The mug of cappuccino brewed to perfection, Samiyah grabbed it off the Nespresso coffee maker and blew lightly at the steam. Claudia entered the kitchenette. "Feeling better this morning?"

Samiyah leaned against the counter. "If by better you mean shifting my focus from my mother to something else then yes, much better."

Claudia smirked, "Oh honey, you guys will come to an understanding at some point, but you know she is set in her ways. Hey, I told you at the beginning of the week not to get your hopes up about her changing. So, when you called me last night fussing, I just sat back with a glass of   wine   and   listened."

"Yeah, I don't want to talk about it. In other news, you have yet to show me this dress you're wearing to the benefit tonight."

"Ah yes," Claudia kissed her fingertips one at a time. "It's magnificent! Samiyah giggled.

"Why haven't I seen it?"

"I haven't seen yours. I sent you a photo!"

"Actually, you were on the verge of sending me a picture when you found out you and Jonas were front page news."

Samiyah frowned. "Oh yeah. Wait, you didn't see it when we were moving?"

"No ma'am, I was too focused on that fine stallion of a man to notice anyway."

Samiyah cut her eyes.

"What?" Claudia asked.

"Must you be so thirsty for a man, where's your independence?"

Claudia gawked, "Says the person who's been married for the last five years. That independence ran out the door when I decided to keep it real with myself. As long as I'm single, I'll be that, but I long to be dependent on someone. Besides you would say that after everything you've been through."

Selena Strauss floated into the room. "Mrs. Manhattan, you have a visitor." Samiyah checked her watch. "My first appointment isn't until nine thirty."

"He's not on your schedule."

"Who is it, Ms. Strauss?"

"Mr. Manhattan."

Samiyah held back an eye roll; her jaw now clinching. She looked to Claudia. "You wouldn't happen to have some whiskey I can drop in this cappuccino, would you?"

Claudia stifled a guffaw as she watched Samiyah leave the kitchen. Inside her office, David sat with his legs traversed, be-suited with perfect posture. Claudia closed her door and sat her cappuccino on the cherry oak wood desk.

"There is nothing of yours left at the house, I forwarded my ring by way of USPS, and the garage has been cleared out."

He stared at her for longer than she liked. Samiyah sat in her swiveled chair her arms coming to rest on the desk. Lightly her fingers began a slow tap, that was her own silent way of saying, anything else?

"You changed your hair." He said.

Samiyah arched an eyebrow. "I wouldn't call it changed, I merely cut the front so a bang would hang above my eyes. The rest is still long and wavy just the way you hate it." She smirked.

His posture buckled and he relaxed in his seat loosening his tie. "It's hard for me to do this."

"To do what?" An ink pen was in her hand now. It swayed back and forth as she tapped it on her desk but kept her focus on him. His eyes went to it, a vein popping up on his forehead. He wanted to scold her, but he let it go.

"It's hard for me to be here."

"Why are you here, David?"

He averted her stare taking his attention to the glass window pane behind her. "I'm sorry."

She inched forward slightly. "Say what?"

His eyes met hers. "I'm sorry." It was clearer this time. There was shame on his face but determination in his eyes.

"What are you sorry for? What's done is done. I'm over it, I've moved on."

"With that guy who was at the house. That's who you've moved on with?"

He was jealous. Samiyah would've rejoiced in the feeling, but honestly, she didn't care. "Is that all you wanted to say, you're sorry? Apology accepted, now get out." Her hand had ceased its tap dance and was now clenched around the writing tool in a fist.

"Baby."

"No," she shook her head vehemently. "That's one thing you will not do. Get out."

"I know I messed up."

Her mouth opened and closed. She reached forward and hit a button on her desktop phone.

"Security." They answered.

"Could you come and escort Mr. Manhattan out of the building. Make sure he makes it to his car safely, please." She released the button.

"Samiyah don't do this. You said it yourself, our marriage deserves another chance."

"Newsflash David, we are divorced. So, the words 'our marriage' no longer apply when talking about you and me. And another thing. I don't know what's happened between you and your little girlfriend, but I don't want any part of it." There was a knock, and her door swung open. Two security guards pulled up in front of him. He rose closing the lone button on his jacket.

"This had nothing to do with me and her and everything to do with me and you. I can see myself out."

He left her office with security behind him. Selena Strauss stuck her head in. "Mrs. Manhattan your 9:30 is here."

"Send her in, Ms. Strauss."

Jonas had been calling Samiyah since she'd left her townhouse at the beginning of the week. He understood the scene in his office was misleading, but she wasn't even giving him a chance.

The cellphone in his lap chimed, and he answered without hesitation. "How can I help you?"

"I'm glad that you asked." At the sound of Kevin's voice, annoyance took root.

"Let's meet in person. I have a bonus for your corporation once you agree to this fight."

"Kevin, it's never going to happen."

"Just hear me out, what do you have to lose? You know you'll win. Adding an extra one hundred fifty million dollars to your bank account has to be tempting."

"If this were five years ago, maybe, but not now. That's what being retired means."

"That's why this is an off the book fight. No one has to know about it but the people involved."

Jonas cracked a smile. "My refusal has nothing to do with people knowing."

"What does it have to do with? Inquiring minds want to know."

Jonas didn't respond.

"Listen if you'd rather discuss it in person let's set a date. I promise you won't regret it."

"I have no desire to talk about my reasons for not participating. I'm sure you can find someone else who's a good fighter. After all, it is your specialty."

"I appreciate the faith you have in me but your selling yourself short if you think I can find someone better then you. I'm sure if you came out of retirement you could beat the current champion."

Jonas smirked. "I've gotta go."

"Wait, listen, let's have a conversation. I'll be at the old gymnasium tomorrow, trust me you'll change your mind once you get there."

Jonas ended the call. The limo pulled up in front of the Hilton Hotel and stopped. The door opened to a flash of photographers taking shot after shot not wanting to miss an angle as he stepped out.

"Mr. Rose, look left please!" One photographer yelled. "Mr. Rose turn to your right!"

He paused long enough to give the photographers a few still frames before tilting his head with a gentle smile and moving forward down the red carpet. The lobby was designed in a beautiful array of purple and white solidifying the March of Dimes signature colors.

"Jonas Alexander Rose," a man said approaching him, his hand held out for a shake. "It's good to see you in attendance."

"Mr. Mayor," Jonas said accepting his handshake. "Always a pleasure."

"Have you ever thought about running for an electoral seat?"

"Not once," Jonas responded.

"Why not? I think you're just what Chicago needs to shake things up a bit."

"You might be right," Jonas flashed a signature smile.

"Well if it isn't Jonas Alexander Rose," came another voice. The men turned to see Jaden and Jordan Rose approach. The brothers smiled shaking hands pulling each other in for hugs.

"Mr. Mayor," they said acknowledging his presence. "I thought you wouldn't make it for a moment big brother. The auction is getting ready to start."

"I was saying the same thing," the mayor asserted. "Let's find our seats, shall we? I'm looking forward to outbidding one of you fellas tonight," he said with a humorous sneer.

"This should be interesting," Jordan said rubbing his hands together.

"Where's your partner's in crime, Jordan?" Jonas asked. No sooner than he'd mentioned them, Jonathon, Julian, Josiah and Jacob made their entrance.

"Speak of the devils," Jaden said.

"Well if it isn't a few good men," Jonas said referring to Julian. Julian was the most sought after international male model and founder of A Few Good Men male modeling agency. They slapped hands and reached out hugging and greeting each other.

"How's business, fellas?"

"Better than ever," Josiah said. The men agreed.

"I can't complain," Jonathon replied. "My security firm is growing, and I hear you're not doing so bad yourself big brother.

With a sparkling gleam in his eye, Jonas confirmed, "Not doing too bad at all. Let's get this show on the road."

Chapter Twenty Two

The men left the lobby and made their way into the ballroom. Chandeliers, upscale furnishings, and beautiful bouquets stretched around the room as far as the eye could see. The who's who of Chicago was in the building including but not limited to, the Mayor, the Governor, city council members, actors, singers, authors and more. Every woman in the building had turned their total focus to the seven gorgeous men; no doubt hoping to be on one of their arms by the end of the night. Some women didn't even wait for an invite. They made their approach with confidence in their strides.

Jonas surveyed the room with a strong sense of awareness. There was a huge crowd at the event, but it didn't stop his eyes from landing on her, standing farther across the room than he would've like. Jonas hid his surprise behind his focused observation as he willed her to meet his stare.

Samiyah was on her second Mai Tai. "How many of those are you going to drink," Claudia asked her.

"I'm sorry, are you my chaperone because the last time I checked, I'm an adult."

"Since the moment you signed those papers you've been drinking."

"Excuse me, but it's not like I didn't drink before."

"Yeah, but it was like twice a year."

"If you must know, this has nothing to do with David and everything to do with my nerves."

"It's okay girl, it's just one date. You're not an escort, and look on the bright side? This event not only helps a worthy cause that you feel strongly about, but it also gave us the opportunity to network. I already have a few respectable clients lined up from this event. I'm sure you do, too."

It was true. Samiyah's beauty struck any man that saw her coming to the extent that they went along with whatever she was saying. Some who already had financial advisors offered to use her services insisting they could always use a second opinion. Samiyah wasn't new to flattery, but it still tickled her how some men fawned over her. In Samiyah's mind, she was as regular as regular could be. Samiyah turned her back to the bar and sighed bringing her Mai Tai to her lips. With a sudden change of energy in the room, her eyes shifted to the double door entrance.

Immediately a heated flare welled from her feet rising through her legs, then thighs, wrapping around her midsection glazing its way to the crown of her head. An audible sound left her mouth at the sight of Jonas Alexander Rose. His steely gaze ripped through her, and Samiyah felt her breathing becoming erratic. The Mai Tai in her hand was forgotten as she watched his long strides bring him across the room. Like the sexiest marching band she'd ever seen, all six of his brothers followed him in a glorious sync that couldn't be broken. It seemed like a lifetime for him to get to her, with women stepping into their path and men looking to hold a conversation; neither coming close to halting his advances.

Samiyah didn't know when she put her drink down but it was no longer in her hand. Once Jonas was closer, Samiyah got a good look at the gorgeousness that was all male, and his splendor oozed masculinity. The all-black tailored suit fit his well-built, powerful frame in the finest fashion.

Now standing in front of Samiyah, Jonas reached out and bent slightly placing a warm kiss on the back of her hand. "Mademoiselle, you are... sublime," he said; his voice thick and sexy. "I had no idea you'd be at this event."

It took Samiyah a second to remember she was mad at him but when it came to her, she quickly removed her hand. "My intentions were to tell you a few weeks ago, but you were occupied." She said.

"We should talk."

"Now is not the time to discuss it, don't you think?"

His eyes gleamed and sat low never leaving hers. His lips were moist and screaming to taste the details of hers and every nerve ending in Samiyah's body was on edge. It took sheer willpower to cut her eyes from Jonas to the rest of the men occupying their space.

Good evening Jaden," Samiyah acknowledged. Jaden was the only brother she'd been formally introduced to.

"Hello beautiful," Jaden answered receiving a stern glare from Jonas.

"Excuse me, where are my manners, Samiyah these are my brothers, Jonathon, Julian, Jordan, Josiah, Jacob, and you've already met Jaden. Fellas this is Samiyah Manhattan, Co-owner of S & M Financial Advisors and this is..."

"Claudia Stevens, my business partner," Samiyah said finishing his sentence. There are two other employees here with us Selena Strauss and Octavia Davenport, but they're backstage getting ready for the auction."

The men greeted the women and Claudia knew she was in male model heaven. With the men surrounding them, Samiyah and Claudia were envied by every woman in attendance, even those already partnered with dates. Jonas couldn't pull his eyes away from Samiyah. The all white evening gown she wore fit every curve that she held. The dress gave Samiyah a mermaid fit at the top that sprouted into a small flare at her ankles.

Pearl studs bejeweled her ears, and Samiyah's hair sat up in the tightest bun on her head. It showcased her neckline that was covered with a white pearl necklace. There was no doubt that she was the most stunning woman in the building tonight and Jonas didn't need to case the place to come to that conclusion.

A man stepped to the podium and cleared his throat. It was only then that Jonas looked away.

"May I have your attention, please. Thank you, ladies and gentlemen for attending this March of Dimes auction. I hope you brought your wallets because tonight we have a beautiful array of lovely ladies who are helping us raise money for this wonderful charity. So, without further ado, let's get started."

Applause rose around the room, and Jonas glanced back toward Samiyah, but she was gone.

Backstage Samiyah got her nerves together. Jonas had thrown her entire equilibrium off.

"Girl those men are built for the Gods, honey," Claudia said. "When you stood up to leave I thought you would have to pull me kicking and screaming for a minute." She gave Samiyah a serious look. "And Jaden..." she kissed the tip of her fingers and shook her head. "Girl, there are no words to describe him."

"There are no words needed; I was there remember?"

Samiyah and Claudia stood behind three other women in a line that lingered through the dressing room. When one woman left the stage, another entered. Slowly but surely, they were making their way to the front. Amanda stood behind Claudia dressed down in a beige sequined evening gown that hung just to her knees. No doubt she was trying to impress Jonas. Her matching accessories sparkled, and she wore a dark red lipstick.

"Good luck, ladies," Amanda spoke to Samiyah and Claudia. Samiyah dipped her head, "Same to you," she responded out of courtesy.

"I'm sure I'll have a pleasant evening; you ladies make sure you do the same. I hear there are six other brothers to choose from."

Claudia felt a strange vibe coming from Amanda but decided not to explore it. Samiyah gave a phony smile. "So there is," she said.

Now at the top of the line, the woman coming off the stage was squealing with delight having received the highest bid.

"Two hundred and fifty thousand dollars, can you believe it!" She danced past the women all too happy to get to her date.

When the auctioneer called Samiyah's name, she stepped from behind the curtain and glided gracefully to the center of the stage. The spotlight held on her illuminating everything she wore.

"We'll start the bidding at thirty thousand dollars."

Without hesitation men started bidding on her, more than Samiyah had anticipated. Her eyes scanned the room for Jonas but didn't find him.

"Sixty-five thousand," a man said.

"Seventy-five," said another.

"Eighty-five," came another.

"One hundred thousand."

Samiyah followed the familiar voice, her eyes landing on Dr. Blake Sanchez."

She couldn't help but smirk. The doctor was just as insistent as someone else she knew, but at least if he won the bid she would be on a date with someone she recognized, and his money would go to a good cause. Another guy chimed in.

"One hundred and fifty thousand." Came a voice from a prominent surgeon from an opposing hospital.

The boys went back and forth challenging each other until the bid had reached, Three hundred forty thousand dollars.

The surgeon bidding against Dr. Blake Sanchez paused and stole another look at Samiyah. She gave a fleeting smile, and the surgeon placed another bid.

"Four hundred thousand."

All attention went back to Dr. Sanchez, and he didn't bat an eye. "Five hundred thousand," the doctor said setting his sights on Samiyah. He offered her a small smile. Sanchez knew the surgeon wouldn't bid behind that.

"Five hundred thousand going once, twice..."

"One million dollars."

The audience sharp gasps could be heard around the room as all in attendance were stunned by the enormous generosity of the bid. Samiyah, equally stunned covered a hand over her chest as everyone in the room turned to the voice that spoke out. Jonas stepped out of the darkness with purpose in his eyes that lured Samiyah in and took her breath away.

"One million dollars going once, twice..." The auctioneer dropped his gavel and yelled, "Sold!"

A thunderous round of applause drummed throughout the ballroom as Jonas made his way to the stage. Instead of waiting for her to join him, he went to claim Samiyah holding her in a spellbinding gaze as his stride brought him to her. Jonas was done holding back, and Samiyah would know for sure it was her that he wanted. When his fingers grazed her chin, Samiyah shivered, and Jonas never hesitated to bring his lips down on hers into a steamy, exotic kiss. Samiyah stood cemented where she was taking in every bit of his fiery passion. They never noticed the flashes from the cameras, and the whistles from the men, and frankly, they didn't care.

Chapter Twenty Three

"You were right. I have been holding back." Jonas sat on the ottoman facing Samiyah. After the explosive kiss at the auction, he'd taken her hand and fled the event. He drove straight to his downtown penthouse not wanting to leave her side for a moment.

She looked on inquisitively. "You must understand something about me Samiyah. I've never had to speak about my personal life with anyone."

"So you've never been in a relationship or even had a close friend?"

"I have acquaintances. Besides my brothers who already know my past, I have no need to be close to anyone." He peered at her. "As for women, I've never let one get close enough to reveal myself completely."

Samiyah shifted in her seat. She still wore her evening gown, but it wasn't the dress that made her a little uncomfortable. The look on his beautiful face now was sturdy and rigid, almost as if it pained him to release whatever it was that he held pinned up inside.

He loosened the tie around his neck. "My mother and I were very close. Being my father's first born came with many responsibilities. On the eve of my mother's thirty-fifth birthday, my father left me in charge of the house.

Whenever he did this he would say, son, you're the man of the house until I get back. Look after your mother and brothers. I would always respond, I'm on it, sir.'"

Samiyah smiled a bit imaging Jonas as a young boy wanting to make his father proud.

"My mother was making dinner for us, and she needed flour from the store. Jonas, she said, 'I need you to run down to the market and get a bag of flour. Don't take too long now, hurry back.' He leaned forward resting his forearms on his thighs never breaking his eye contact with her.

"She placed a kiss on my forehead and gave me some bills, and I was gone. Back then, I had a ten-speed bicycle I liked to call the hedgehog after the animated game Sonic the Hedgehog; primarily because I rode it at lightning speed. That night, I took my time going to the store. When I got there, some neighborhood kids were lingering around. One of the guys challenged me, telling me his bike was faster than mine. I could never bow out of a challenge, so I accepted.

His face lit up. "We took off down the road and as sure as my name is Jonas Rose I smoked him, left him in the wind, boy was he mad. I laughed all the way back to the store. After getting the flour, I headed back to the house with a chip on my shoulder and a smile on my face. I couldn't wait to tell my younger brothers the story."

"I rode into the driveway jumping off my bike before it came to a complete stop. The first thing I noticed was the front door. Not only was it unlocked it was hanging open with an imprint in the front door like it had been kicked in."

His face darkened. "I could hear Julian crying loud, so I rushed to him to see what was wrong. He was only eight years old. When I found him, he was standing over my mother." His jaw tightened. "She was lying in a pool of her own blood. She'd been shot."

"Jonas—" Samiyah said.

"Let me finish," he spoke closing his eyes tight then reopening them reliving the memory. "I remember dropping down to my knees and shaking her. I felt around her neck for a pulse but couldn't tell if she had one. I ran to the phone and called the police. The dispatcher tried to keep me on the line but I couldn't, I needed to find the rest of my brothers."

Samiyah could tell he was gone by the faraway look in his eyes. Although they were trained on her, he was no longer present.

"I grabbed Julian by the hand and went to my father's cabinet where he kept his guns. He'd taught me how to shoot them outside in the backyard and on hunting expeditions. I grabbed one, made sure it was loaded, and went room to room. I found my sister's in their crib sleeping soundly. They were newborns barely two weeks old. I came out their room and closed the door and went in search of my brothers with Julian trailing me. I found Jaden unconscious by the back door a gun laying at his side. I called out to him, but Jaden didn't respond, so I fell to my knees to check his pulse.

My heart was beating so fast and I feared he was dead. I ran back to the kitchen and got the pitcher of water my mother kept in the refrigerator and poured it on his face. He woke up with a heavy groan and I could tell he'd been hit over the head from the way it was swelling on one side. Jaden! I yelled, Are you okay? He just groaned and groaned then finally he said, 'did you get em?"

No, I just got back. You have to get up. You have to help me find Jonathon, Jordan, Jacob, and Josiah!

Jaden was still in a daze, but alert enough to mention they went to the lake. No sooner than he said it, I spotted them walking through the back yard laughing and pushing each other.

Someone yelled, Freeze! And I turned around with the gun lifted in my hand. Chicago P.D. had their guns trained on me. 'Put the weapon down son,' they said. It took me a second to snap out of it, but I dropped the gun."

Samiyah moved from her place on the sofa and crouched between his legs on her knees trying to soothe him from the memory.

"We were questioned over and over again. Jaden being two years younger than me had tried to stop the intruder. He'd done the same thing I did which was grab one of our father's guns. Unfortunately, he was knocked out before he could use it. My mother," he held his tongue, "she died."

"It was ruled a robbery-homicide."

"Jonas, I'm so sorry for asking. I never meant to make you relive such a horrible incident. Please accept my apologies." She reached to touch his face, caressing him with her soft hand.

"You deserve to know," he said. He reached for the scotch that was sitting next to him and knocked it back. "The intruders were caught some days later with items they'd stolen from the house. But the one thing I could never have back was gone forever. Needless to say, I blamed myself for it. I should've never left the house that evening. I was in charge."

"You couldn't have known that was going to happen. If you'd been there you might have died yourself."

"Then so be it. I was in charge."

He gritted his teeth, and Samiyah's eyes watered. "For the next few years, everything in my life changed. I started acting out in school, my grades dropped, I picked fights." He poured another glass and took a huge gulp.

"My father seemed to think I needed to find a way to let go of my frustrations. Imagine that? A teenager and already I felt like the world was on my shoulders. When I was seventeen, he took me to the gym and introduced me to Ned Clayborn. 'Son,' he said, Ned's going to help you relieve some of that stress.

He put gloves on my fists and put me in front of a punching bag. For the first couple of weeks, I didn't take anything Ned was saying seriously. I just showed up and repeatedly hit the punching bag, over and over. One day he walked up to me and said, 'how would you feel about fighting in a match?' I was cocky, arrogant, and I told him I'd win hands down. He said follow me. We walked over to a match that was going on in the center part of the gym. I observed the fighter's movements, completely lost in a trance. Ned was watching me, then he said, 'If you follow my instructions you'll be better than them.'

From that day forward I was doing whatever he said. He had me doing everything physical. I jumped rope for hours some days. He put me in front of the punching bag and yell, 'stand up straight your spine shouldn't be bent, forget everything you saw on TV or heard about boxing and listen to me.'"

"And I did. My training became fierce. Night and day, I was there seven days a week. My grades began to improve. I wasn't picking random fights anymore, and my attitude at home was much better. That's all my dad cared about. He saw me spiraling and thought boxing would help, and he was right. I trained for years before I had my first match and when I did, I came out the victor. My father and brothers were proud and so was I. Boxing became my new love. I fought for ten years straight never losing one fight and profited handsomely from it."

"That's amazing," Samiyah said.

"I never expected to win as much, but it was a combination, of skill, dedication, training, and stress. Anytime I stepped in the ring I relieved the stress from that day, and every year on my mother's death date I made sure I had a match."

"Sounds like you had a good thing going," Samiyah said.

"It was a great thing."

"So, why'd you retire?"

His face fell grim again. "On November 13, 2009, I was set to fight D'Angelo Santarus. On the night of the fight, the crowd was huge. The announcer called us both out one at a time. We entered the ring. The match started, and we tapped gloves and separated. It took one round and ten minutes for me to get a K.O., which in boxing terms is a knockout. It was the quickest fight of my life. The crowd cheered and went crazy."

Again, he traveled back to the night in question. "I was declared the winner. D'Angelo was still on the ring floor. His trainers and medical team had surrounded him. I watched from the sidelines as they checked him out. I heard one man say I can't find a pulse. The emergency team came in and worked on him until they found one. From there they airlifted him to the closest hospital. Before I left the changing room, I asked Ned how he was doing. His face was long and somber, and he didn't respond. Ned, I said, he looked up at me. Ned said, he was pronounced dead at nine fifty-three p.m."

Samiyah gasped, and Jonas fell silent. He reached for his glass and took the final sip of his scotch and continued.

"To make matters worse, rumors were going around that D'Angelo didn't weigh enough to fight me. His handler had fabricated his weight because he thought he had a winner. But he wasn't blamed for it, I was. People thought I was showing off and took things too far by fighting him when I didn't have a clue. I fought for two years after that before I finally decided to give it up. The nightmares I had were extreme. Not only was I seeing D'Angelo but my mom, too, and boxing was no longer my haven."

He looked down in her face his eyes glossy, his jaw tight. "So you see, my love, I'm a broken man. It took a lot of counseling for the nightmares to stop and the pain to lift and I've never talked about it until now."

Tears rolled down Samiyah's cheeks. She felt utterly horrible for bringing up his past. "You couldn't have known," he said reading her mind and seeing the guilt on her face.

"I'm so, so, sorry..." he captured her lips with his, her hands caressed his face and their kiss intensified. Jonas pulled Samiyah into his lap, and they consumed each other. Her hands moved to his tie completely undoing it; working her fingers down the buttons on his shirt. It opened easily, and in haste, she removed it off of his brawny shoulders and muscular arms.

He unzipped the back of her gown and peeled it off of her smooth mocha skin. Clothes went flying across the room, and Samiyah eagerly jumped back on his lap kissing his neck and shoulders as tears continued to flow from her eyes. She felt entirely responsible for making him relive such a horrible time in his life, and she wanted to make it all better.

"I love you, I love you," she repeated as she kissed his skin. He pulled her face to his and worked her hips on him. Samiyah shut her eyes tight.

"Look at me," he commanded. Her eyes opened with sadness still in them. "I love you too, Samiyah," he rotated her hips grinding them into him. "Don't close your eyes, stay with me."

Samiyah placed her feet on the ground and moved up in down in steady rotation, picking up a momentum that had tears streaming down both of their faces. Their passionate kisses picked up once again and his strong arms encircled her, holding on so tight they became one. Samiyah's head fell back, and she moaned in an overabundance of pleasure.

His lips dropped to her breasts, and he licked and sucked her nipples like he'd never taste a piece of chocolate before. Samiyah rode and rode until they both erupted in volcanic fashion, their bodies succumbing to the desire that overtook them. With her body still trembling against him, he rose, and she wrapped her legs around him as he carried her into the master bedroom. With the moon casting night light across the bed, they made love and whispered sweet endearments to each other until they lacked any energy.

At four a.m., Jonas shifted in his bed and was awakened by the emptiness that settled there. He slid up to his elbows and looked around the room. The sliding doors to the patio was peeled back, and the moonlight cast a shadow across the floor. He removed the sheets and crept to the balcony.

"Is everything okay?"

Samiyah stepped into his arms. "You were not supposed to wake up."

"If you want me to sleep, you have to stay with me. What's on your mind, love?"

"Everything, well..." she peered back into the night. "Us mostly. My mother would never approve. She's very hard on men. She thinks there's not a good one left alive. It's understandable I guess, but sometimes I wish she would just give someone a chance." He rubbed her shoulders.

"Maybe she needs to be in the presence of good men to feel like they still exist."

Samiyah cackled. "It's not like I just know a gang of good men I can introduce her to."

"I may know a few."

She turned to him. "You're not insisting your brothers are you. They are too young! She would rip them to shreds."

"Yeah right, I know a cougar when I see one."

Samiyah punched him in the gut, and he pretended to be hurt by her jab. "Okay, I deserved that."

"Yes, you did," she said matter of factly.

"No, I only meant maybe she needs to experience what it is like to be around good men."

"Well, I don't know how you plan to make that happen. If I know anything about my mother, she is impossible when it comes to men."

"We'll see, in the meantime come back to bed." He pulled her inside and shut the door. It didn't take long for them to start up another round of love making.

Chapter Twenty Four

Sunday morning came quicker than Jonas cared for, especially since he'd spent half of the early morning making love to Samiyah. The ringing of his cell phone eventually pulled him out of his complete rest. He tried to slide his arms away from around her, when Samiyah snuggled in tightly, pressing her butt against him. He grew instantly hard and decided to stay put. He put his lips up to her cheek and laid soft kisses on them.

"Mmmm," Samiyah said.

"Good morning, love."

A smile lit up her face. "You tried to get away, but I got you this time." Her voice was soft and sweet.

His brows furrowed and she turned around. "The first time we made love you disappeared, and I woke up in bed alone."

"It was not my intent to leave you alone."

"I know, but I'm just glad I caught you this time."

He smiled and moved some hair out of her eyes. "So you did," he said gently.

His phone rang again. "Go ahead but come right back." She instructed.

"Yes ma'am." He said making it to his phone and back to her in record time.

She snuggled back under him as he brought his phone to his ear. "Yes sir," he answered.

"Hello son, I didn't wake you, did I?"

"As a matter of fact, you did."

"Well, you can stand to get woken up a time or two by your old man."

"That I can."

"Your brothers are in town. Of course you know this since you're all over the Chicago Tribune. I want you all to come over tonight for dinner and bring that beauty of yours you were all over, too."

Jonas pulled the phone back and glanced at it, slowly he put it back to his ear, "Which beauty would that be pop," he joked.

Samiyah peered at him, and he grinned. "The one you're in love with." His father said.

In all seriousness, Jonas said, "What makes you think I'm in love, pop?"

"I was in love with your mom for thirty years. I know what love looks like, and it's all in your face on that paper. Now stop giving me a hard time and bring her I said."

"Yes, sir."

"I'm calling Jaden to tell him to bring the one he was with, too."

Jonas raised a brow. "This should be interesting."

"Alright son, I won't keep you."

"I'll see you later, pop."

They disconnected the call, and he tossed his cell to the side.

"Which beauty?" Samiyah questioned.

"Were you ear hustling?

"You only said it loud enough so I could hear." She was giving him attitude.

Jonas burst into laughter, and she pouted. "Come here girl. You know I was messing with you and him for that matter. He wants to meet you."

She lit up. "Wait, how does he know?"

"Apparently, we're today's news."

Samiyah groaned and buried her head in his chest.

"It's okay love. You'll get used to it."

Martha Jean slipped three grocery bags onto her wrist and reached for three more to place on her other wrist.

"Please let me help you with that."

She yelped turning to his voice. "Boy, you scared me half to death!"

"I'm so sorry, please accept my apology, that was not my aim."

"Well, what do you expect if you sneak up on an old lady like that!"

Jonas berated her with a charming smile. "You're hardly old ma'am." He took the bags out of her hands.

"You can run that game on my daughter, but not on me."

"I don't play games. Like I told your daughter when we first met, I'm straightforward about my intentions."

She folded her arms. "And exactly what are your intentions, Mr. Rose?"

"I'm in love with your daughter."

There weren't many things that could cause Martha Jean to be speechless, but this was one of them. She blinked several times trying to wrap her mind around what he just said.

"How could you be in love with her? How long have you guys known each other?"

"I know, it's been about two months now. I realize how impossible that must sound."

"More like insane," she said shaking her head. She walked to her front door and unlocked it. They stepped inside, and she showed him to the kitchen. He placed the bags down on her table and faced her.

"When I met your daughter, she was nursing a broken heart. Her marriage had just ended, and misery was all over her face. Even though at the time I didn't know the reason for her sadness I worried about her." He smirked. "She was hot headed and didn't want to be bothered, but circumstances threw us on the same path. Since then I haven't been able to shake this intemperate feeling of protection for her."

Martha twisted her lips.

"I know," Jonas held his hands up in surrender, "she doesn't need my protection, but that doesn't negate the fact that I feel the way I do. She's on a mission to prove that she doesn't need nor want a man."

Martha went to speak.

"Before you say anything let me finish."

She closed her mouth and shifted her weight from one foot to the other.

"Within this short time that I've known Samiyah, I've learned to love her smile, her passion for others, her strength in times of despair, and her spunkiness. I've seen her laugh, cry, and love. She's touched me in many ways no one ever has. And I don't intend to let her get away."

"Why are you telling me all of this," Martha questioned.

"She cares about what you think of her, and even though she won't say it, she wants you to be proud of her."

"I am proud of her."

He pinned her with a slight glare. "You're judgmental, and it's fine if you want to spend the rest of your life alone, but she won't. I'll make sure of that. I respect that you're her mother, but I won't allow you to break her down with spiteful words and unenthusiastic rhetoric. Am I clear?"

Instead of feeling like slapping him across the face, Martha was amused and shocked. He sure was in love with Samiyah, and she didn't resent either of them for it.

"Loud and clear," she said. "Did Samiyah send you over here?"

"No, she has no idea I know where you live."

"How do you know where I live?"

He smirked. "I have my ways. It's nothing you should be worried about."

"Un huh," she said. "Are you finished reading me my rights?"

"I would love to get to know you."

"Why? Don't you got a mother of your own?"

He was determined to have patience with her. "Actually, my mother passed some time ago."

Martha's face fell. "I'm sorry. I have a bad habit of saying the first thing that comes to mind." She pulled out her electronic cigarette and began to smoke. "Sure, if you're going to be in my daughter's life I guess we better get to know one another. Besides, you don't seem so bad anyway."

A light chuckle left him. "I'm sure you're not too bad yourself." Martha smirked, then they burst into laughter.

"We're having dinner at my father's house tonight. Would you like to join us?"

She inhaled her vaporizer. "Who's cooking?"

"Norma, our housekeeper. She's been a part of the family for years. She makes a mean meatloaf, too."

"Hmph, I'll be the judge of that."

"You have to be on your best behavior."

"I'll do no such thing."

Jonas gave her a warning look.

She sighed, "Fine, have it your way."

"I am so siked!" Claudia squealed.

"Girl that man of yours knows how to make a scene." She shook her head. "The place was buzzing when he whisked you off that stage. I mean you didn't even stick around to find out how well I did."

"I'm sorry girl; I was in just as much shock as everyone else. How did you do?"

"Oh girl, I don't blame you honey, I would've left too if it had been me." Claudia laughed. "But girl, rather than talk about how much was bid on me, let's talk about who."

"Okay, who?" Samiyah could barely get the words out before Claudia squealed again.

"Jaden Rose!" Claudia did a tap dance around her living room. "We didn't leave in the same style you guys did, but we did spend the rest of the night in a quiet corner getting to know one another. He is so handsome and down to earth. Who knew?"

Samiyah was happy for her friend. If Jaden was anything like Jonas she was in good hands.

"His dad wants to meet me. At first Jaden was like, you don't have to come I know we're not in the meet your parent's stage yet." She squealed again. "He said yet!"

Samiyah laughed, "I'm going to be there as well, it seems his dad wanted to meet us both."

"We can ride together, right?" Claudia said hopeful.

"Actually, Jonas was going to pick me up, but I'll tell him I'm riding with you."

"Perfect! What should I wear? I have no idea."

"Nothing fancy like what you wore last night. Make sure you're comfortable but sexy. You don't want to look desperate or like a hussy, but you do want to look delicious."

Another squeal came through the phone, and Samiyah laughed.

"Oh, girl that heffa who was standing behind me in line was horrified when Jonas bid on you. You'd think she was his girl or something the way she acted."

Samiyah thought back to Amanda, "Yeah, that's his assistant. Apparently, they had made previous plans. He was supposed to bid on her, but that was before he knew I was also attending the auction."

"Poor girl," Claudia said. "I was getting strange vibes from her anyway. She'll be alright."

"What did she say?"

"It's not what she said, it's what she did. Girl, she threw this temper tantrum like she was a teenager then cried her eyes out. She never made it to the stage, not that I know of anyway, unless somebody talked some sense into her. Anyway, I'll be ready at five then I'll be over there to pick you up."

"Okay, see you in a little bit."

When Claudia arrived, Samiyah was walking out of her front door. She climbed into the passenger seat. Claudia inhaled her scent giving the air a little sniff.

"Smells good, what are you wearing?" she asked.

"It's a bath and body works vanilla collection."

Claudia pulled onto the road. "That smells delightful."

"Thanks, are you nervous?" Samiyah asked.

"If you could see the fine hairs on my neck I'm sure they're standing at attention."

Samiyah giggled. "Take some deep breaths meeting his father couldn't be that bad."

"It's not his father I'm worried about. It's all of them fine, gorgeous, scrumptious, brothers, that will be gathered around us with nowhere to run." She fanned herself.

"As if you want to run somewhere," Samiyah quipped.

"I don't girl, I truly don't."

Samiyah laughed again. It took them thirty minutes to get to the house. When they pulled up, the large colonial style home sat on a road on its own, on an acre of land. They pulled into the paved driveway and parked.

"Should we call first?" Claudia wondered.

Samiyah checked her time. It was ten minutes till six, and they were a few minutes early. "I think we should just ring the bell."

They gave their appearances one last check before exiting the car and making their presence known. When the door swung open, and a pair of dark gray eyes stared back, Julian Alexander Rose stood on the other side looking like he'd just stepped out of GQ magazine.

"Good evening ladies," his eyes traveled over them both with a satisfactory gleam. "By all means, come in," he said stepping out of the way.

Chapter Twenty Five

They entered the foyer and were escorted to the dining hall. Julian cleared his throat. "Fellas, we have company."

One by one all eyes turned to them. Claudia almost cursed, and Samiyah was right there with her. Claudia was right, it was a delight to be surrounded by the gorgeous men.

"Hello ladies," they all stated.

"Hey beautiful," Jonas said coming up behind Samiyah; his strong arms immersing her in a tight hug. He leaned slightly placing a barrage of kisses on her cheek.

The intense warmth that took over her when he was near would never get old, and she would revel in it every time. Her face swelled into a blush. "Hey sweetheart."

He turned her around to face him and placed a kiss soft and slow on her lips.

"You know every time I see you two, you're hugged up like that," Jaden said walking up beside Jonas. He turned to Claudia, "Hello, pretty girl."

Her smile lit up. "Hello yourself."

"You ladies are right on time. How are you doing? I'm Christopher Lee Rose," their father said, making an entrance. He reached to pull their hands in for a kiss.

"Hello," they said simultaneously. Heavy footsteps danced down the staircase. "That bathroom is too cute to be left alone. What kind of man decorates a bathroom anyway."

Samiyah gawked at her mother's entrance. Her head whipped around to Jonas, then Christopher, back to her mother. "Mom!"

"Oh, hey baby, it's about time you got here I'm starving. You know it's rude to eat before everybody joins the table, but you were almost one piece of cornbread too late."

Claudia covered her mouth in shocked silence, snickering into her hand. "I had no idea you'd be here." Samiyah didn't know whether to be joyous or horrified.

"I know," Martha lifted an eye to Jonas. "I was invited. Not by you, of course."

Samiyah fumbled out her next words, "I um, had no idea you would want to come and I was also invited but it great to have you here." She pulled her in for a hug. Martha laid kisses on her face.

"Pops, this is Samiyah Manhattan and Claudia Stevens. They own S & M Financial Advisors downtown," Jonas said.

"Business women, I like it, please have a seat. Your mother and I have been getting better acquainted."

Samiyah didn't know what that meant, but she was saying a mental prayer that her mother wouldn't embarrass her. She would decide later whether to kill Jonas or not for inviting her.

Jonas pulled out a chair and Jaden did the same allowing the ladies to sit down comfortably.

"Thank you," Samiyah said to him.

"You're more than welcome."

He took his seat next to hers as the other men around the table did also. The housekeeper, Norma Rodriguez, exited the kitchen. She was a short, stocky lady with salt and pepper hair that was cut right below her ear.

"I'm going to the store, Mr. Rose. I'll be back shortly."

Christopher peered at her. "I haven't been Mr. Rose in years. What has gotten into you today woman," he said.

Jonas slipped out of his chair and went to her, pulling her in for a hug. "Hello Norma, every time I see you it looks as if you're getting younger."

"Sure, fifty-seven years younger," she chuckled, and he grinned; placing a quick kiss on her cheek. "Now Mr. Rose don't start. I'll call you want I want to, sometimes." She turned and went out the door.

"I hope you ladies brought your appetites because Norma cooked a big dinner like she always does when we get together for family meals. She loves cooking for me, but she really loves cooking for them."

"That's because she practically raised us," Josiah said.

The other men agreed. The table was decorated with silver platters with enclosed tops, utensils, and a glass of water at each seat. Samiyah could smell the aroma of food steaming from beneath the covered china.

"Congratulations, sons," the men turned to their father. "All of you. Each of you has excelled in your professional lives, and your mother would be proud of the men you are today, and so am I."

"We were led by example," Jonas said.

"Yes indeed," Jaden agreed.

"He was alright," Jonathon said. Christopher reached out to smack him on the back of his head. "It was just a joke," Jonathon laughed.

"Let me show you what's funny," He said still swinging.

"You know pops will put you in a headlock. I still can't figure out why you do it to yourself," Jonas said.

"I think he likes those headlocks," Jordan threw in.

"You might be right," Jaden said.

They said a prayer over their food and ate, their conversation light and comical. Their playful banter amused Samiyah, and for a moment she thought about her own isolated childhood. She'd always wanted brothers but never had the chance to experience that life.

Jonas leaned to her and whispered in her ear. "Are you enjoying yourself?"

"Very much so," she turned to him with an elated smile.

He leaned closer and placed a kiss on her lips.

"Baby girl, you look different today," Martha quipped.

"Oh, I had my hair cut in the front. I like the bang, what do you think?" Samiyah took a sip of her water.

"No, that's not it. There's a glow. Are you pregnant?"

Water squirted out of Samiyah's mouth, shocked by her mother's question. She reached for a napkin and patted her mouth and hands where the water had landed.

"Oh, don't be so dramatic," Martha inclined. "It's just a question."

Samiyah's eye averted Christopher. "No mom, I'm not."

"Well have you taken a pregnancy test?"

"Mom, no!"

"Then how do you know you're not?"

"Because I just do," Samiyah huffed.

"Well, I know all too well about that glow. Either you're pregnant or in love so which one is it?"

A heavy blush flooded Samiyah's face. This line of questioning would've been okay if they were alone. But here in the midst of all these men was not the right time, in her opinion.

"You can scratch pregnancy off your list mom." Everyone noticed she didn't answer the second part of Martha's question.

"Alright, I know how to take a hint." Martha went back to her food.

Jonas had become glued to Samiyah. She did say she loved him, but he wanted to know how deep her love went. Was it as erratic and insane as his? Samiyah could feel Jonas' eyes on her. She took another sip of water trying to pull herself together.

"So, when's the wedding?" Christopher asked.

Jonas never took his eyes off Samiyah as he spoke to his father. "I'll let you know."

There was a hushed silence that fell over the table. Samiyah felt like her stomach had just done a back flip. Claudia was clutching her pearls. Martha dropped her fork. All eyes were on him; his brothers trying to make out if he was serious.

Samiyah let out a nervous laugh and rubbed his chin. "May I use your restroom," she asked needing the reprieve.

"I'll show you to it."

Jonas moved from his chair and helped Samiyah out of hers, guiding her through the house.

Chapter Twenty Six

When they reached the bathroom, Jonas stood in the doorway.

"Did I scare you," he asked.

She swallowed visibly. "I just took it as a joke. You and my mother seem to be on a roll tonight. Did you guys conspire on this plan of attack," Samiyah asked playfully.

The desire that burned in his eyes was making her body stir.

"It's no attack I assure you. Would it be funny if I meant it?"

Jonas spoke each word carefully leaning in to place a kiss on her lips. Truth be told, he couldn't get enough of her, and the more he spent time with her, the more he never wanted to leave.

There was a round of laughter coming from the dining hall. "I better hurry or Claudia will swear I left her hanging," Samiyah said avoiding his question.

Jonas grinned taking a step back, and she scurried into the bathroom. At the counter, she held her chest. Her breathing, unstable. Could Jonas have been serious, Samiyah wondered. It was absurd to think she could actually get married when she had only been divorced a couple of months. Samiyah shook her head vehemently. No, it was impossible. It was ridiculous. She would be crazy to even consider such a thing, right? Samiyah stared at her reflection in the mirror. Seconds later the door flung open, and Claudia walked in.

"So, that's how it is, huh? You just leave me with those drop dead gorgeous men?" Claudia placed her hands on her hips. Before Samiyah could respond, she fell out with laughter. "I'm just kidding honey. I loved every second of it."

Samiyah smiled sweetly still trying to clear her thoughts.

"I know one thing, I better be the first to know about a wedding."

Samiyah turned back to her. "What are you talking about? I just celebrated a divorce! Does it look like I'm in the spirit to be talking about a wedding?"

"Oh, honey please, you can't fool me. You've got love written all over you. The both of you do. Why do you think his dad asked?"

"You don't know what you're talking about."

"Oh yeah, well while you were in the bathroom, Jonas came back to the table, and he is by far the finest of them all. If you don't want him, I wouldn't mind taking him off your hands."

"Be my guest," Samiyah said calling her bluff.

Claudia rubbed her hands together. "Oooh, really?" Claudia turned to leave the bathroom licking her lips. Samiyah reached out and grabbed her pulling her back by her collar. Claudia yelped coming face to face with her.

"That's what I thought," Claudia said. "I was just teasing you anyway. I only have eyes for Jaden." She wiggled her brows.

"You've proven your point," Samiyah said through clenched teeth.

"Girl, you're so cute when you're feisty. Did anyone ever tell you that? And are you sure you're not pregnant?"

Samiyah rolled her eyes. "Seriously?"

"It doesn't hurt to ask. At least I didn't do it in front everybody."

"I'm not pregnant; I think I know my own body!"

"Okay if you say so."

"I do say so." Samiyah huffed. They left the bathroom. Back in the dining room, the men were discussing the NBA finals.

"Lebron is the better player, and you know it. If not, he wouldn't have gotten the MVP title," Jordan said.

"You have lost your mind if you think Kyrie Irving wasn't deserving of the MVP award. He dominated in every sense of the game," Jonathon said.

"He may have for the finals, but where was he all year? The MVP award goes to the man who has continuously dominated during the season, not just the finals, and we all know that was Lebron." Jaden said. A round of disagreements and mixed feelings on the subject crowded the space.

"Since we're all keeping it real," Samiyah interjected, curious eyes turned to her, interested in what she had to say. "Steph Curry was the real MVP."

"Awe, nah!" they all said going around the table like a band of fanatics at a live game.

"He doesn't even deserve mentioning since they failed at taking the championship home," Julian stated.

Samiyah and Claudia chimed in on why Steph Curry should've been mentioned and how he is better than Lebron. The conversation lasted another hour and a half before the men decided to let Samiyah win her argument.

"You make an excellent point," Jonas said with a grin on his face.

"There's no use arguing with the women, they always win in the end," their father pointed out. The men shook their heads in agreement, and the ladies laughed.

"Now here's a man with some sense," Martha exclaimed.

One by one the men rose from their seats and cleared the table. Samiyah cruised through the swinging door of the kitchen.

"Please Norma, allow me to help you."

Norma stood at the sink filling it with soapy suds. "Oh no dear, I am perfectly fine doing this myself."

"I'm sure you are, but I can't leave without giving a helping hand. I wasn't raised that way. In my home, if you ate, you washed dishes." The ladies chuckled.

"Ain't that the truth," Martha said making her entrance. Norma turned to her placing one hand on her hip.

"Now, just what do you think you're doing?"

"I just finished clearing off the table. Those men were obviously raised right because they tried to take it off my hands but I'm not having it."

Norma looked from mother to daughter. "Well, they don't make 'em like you ladies anymore."

"Don't get it twisted, Norma. We do this because we want to, not because we should," Martha said.

Samiyah chuckled. "If you'll excuse me, Norma, you can take a load off. I'll be finished with these dishes in no time."

"I'm not used to anyone taking over my kitchen, but I'll make a deal with you."

They looked on expectantly. "I'll load the dishwasher. Ms. Manhattan, you can wash the pots and Ms. Martha Jean, you can dry them and put them in the cabinet."

Jonas, Jonathon, and Julian walked through the door. "So, this is where all the women went. You know this is what we do after meals, what's going on Norma?"

She swatted them, "Not today it seems," she smirked.

"Where's Claudia?" Martha asked.

"Probably wherever Jaden is," Samiyah quipped.

"You would be right," Jonas said. He went to Samiyah drawing her in his arms. She flung soap suds at him and laughed. "Oh, you got jokes, huh? You know you don't have to do this."

"That's what I told her," Norma said.

"Again," Samiyah said, "I know that, but I want to do it. And you'll need to get used to it. Both of you."

"You won't hear me complaining again," Jonas said, his voice so close to her ear she could turn around and bite him.

The women finished their tasks in record time. "Now, that's what I call teamwork," Norma said, impressed.

"Yes!" Samiyah checked her time it was after ten. They left the kitchen. Christopher was speaking to the men.

"Before you leave, I wanted to speak with you all about a hunting trip."

Jonas looked to Samiyah. "Do you mind waiting?"

She grabbed her purse. "It's okay, I'll ride back with Claudia."

"What if I want you to ride with me?" he asked.

She chuckled. "Call me when you're done sweetheart, and if it's not too late, you can come over."

He wiggled his eyebrows, and she laughed. "Promise?" Jonas asked.

"I pinky swear it," Samiyah giggled again.

He walked her to the door with Claudia and Jaden following closely behind them.

"Mom, are you riding with us?"

"If it's alright with Jonas, I'll catch a ride with him. Norma is giving me a tour of the garden."

"Are you sure you don't want to wait," Jonas asked.

She smiled. "Spend some time with your father and your brothers. It's obvious he misses you guys."

He bent and kissed her on the lips. "You're right."

"I'll be waiting for your call."

"I'll hold you to that." Jonas winked, watching her walk to their car.

Safe with Me

Chapter Twenty Seven

In the living room, the men found a seat gathering around their father. Norma handed each of them a small glass of brandy.

"Thank you, Norma," Christopher said.

"You're most welcome, sir."

She took her leave. Christopher brought the glass to his lips taking a sip of the strong liquor. "It's been a long time since we've been hunting. I've been on more fishing trips then I can count with Fred and Sampson. But what I want to do is go on a trip with my boys. So how about it, while you're all in town I'd like to make a day of it."

"Dad you talk like we don't live in Chicago," Jordan said.

"Having a home here and living here is two different things," Christopher responded.

"We're only out of town for extended periods of time when business calls for it," Julian said.

"Which your business calls for it often," Christopher retorted.

"Anytime you want to get together for a trip we're here. Just let us know, and we will clear our schedules," Jonas stated.

His father smiled up at him. "Thank you, son. I appreciate that. Let's do It next week."

"The girls will want to come, too," Jacob added.

"They're just as busy as you all," Christopher said. "It seems I have to schedule appointments with all my children these days. Either way, I've already spoken with Eden and Phoebe. We're going to Saint Lucia at the beginning of the year."

"You are not going on a trip to Saint Lucia without me," Jordan injected.

"Me either," they all began one by one.

Christopher chuckled. "Well, you better make reservations then."

The men all agreed and drank their brandy. "That brings me to my next question." His eyes landed on Jaden. "When do you plan to settle down?" Jaden glanced behind his shoulder then back to his father. The other men in the room snickered. "Even though I was looking at Jaden, I'm talking to all of you." The chuckles stopped immediately.

"Ah, now no one has anything to say."

Jonas rose to his feet.

"Where do you think you're going?" Jordan asked.

"Would you like to accompany me to the restroom little brother?" Jonas winked and left the room.

"Well?" Christopher said not willing to let up.

"How many times do we have to have this conversation?" Josiah questioned.

"Until you answer it."

"What do you expect us to do, online dating?" Jacob inquired.

Christopher shrugged. "Might not be such a bad idea."

Groans jumped from one person to the other. "You're kidding me, right?" Jaden objected.

"I don't think it's such a bad idea." All eyes turned to Jonathon. "What?"

"If you want to date you don't have to market yourself online," Julian confirmed.

"I know where you're going with this." Jonathon walked to the bar poured more brandy then turned to them, "But everyone knows who we are. How can we find someone who's sincere and trustworthy when so many women flock to us because of our social status?"

"I'm glad you asked!" Christopher beamed. More groans went throughout the room.

"Excuse me, fellas," Martha peeked her head into the room.

"Are you ready, Ms. Martha Jean?"

Martha looked around the room for Jonas. "Let me get him for you," Jaden stood happy for the interruption.

"I know it's late and you've got business to attend to in the morning," Martha stated.

Christopher checked the time. "It seems that you're right. Okay boys, we'll resume this conversation later."

As each of them filed out of the room, they gave a quick hug and kiss on Martha's cheek. Taken aback, Martha held a steady grin as the last one reached her.

"Drive safely. I don't suppose the brandy you had here tonight will impair your driving?" Christopher posed it as a question.

The men all grinned. "Not even close." Jonas said appearing out of thin air. "Ready?" he posed the question to Martha.

"Yes."

"Did you like the garden?" Jonas asked.

"It was beautiful."

"You're welcomed to visit it anytime."

"I don't know if Mr. Rose would like that."

"I'm sure he would. He could use the company, trust me."

One by one they trailed out the door. Christopher stood next to Jonas, one hand on his shoulder.

"Son, I was serious at the dinner table earlier. As soon as you set a wedding date, let me know. You know Norma is going to want to help out."

"What makes you think Samiyah wants to marry me, pop? She just recently got divorced?"

"Because she loves you just as much as you love her. Any woman in her right mind would be lucky to have you as their husband and time waits for no one. Who wrote the rule book on how long you have to court someone before you marry them? Now go get her."

"I hope you're right," Jonas said.

Jonas didn't know when it happened, but he'd fallen in love with Samiyah and God help him if she didn't feel the same.

On his way to the car, Jonas dialed Samiyah's number and waited for her to answer.

Claudia pulled out of the Rose's parking lot adjusting her rearview mirror. The street was pitch dark since the house sat on its own road for a couple of miles. Claudia turned her high beam lights on.

"Why is his father's house in such a desolate part of town?" Claudia asked.

"It's the home they grew up in, and it has memories of their mother there. He'll probably never leave it."

"Is their mother alive, what's the story behind that?" Claudia asked.

Samiyah thought back to what Jonas had shared with her. Even though Claudia was her best friend the information seemed so personal that she wasn't sure if she should tell it.

"No, she's not." Was all she said.

"What happened to her?"

"You'll have to ask Jaden the next time you see him." Samiyah wiggled her eyebrows.

Speaking Jaden's name brought a broad smile to Claudia's face. "What makes you think I'll be seeing him again?"

"Oh please, you know you'll be seeing that man again."

"He didn't ask me out, and unlike your man, he didn't make any promises to call."

"That doesn't mean he won't."

Claudia was hopeful, even though she'd only had one night of pleasant conversation with him, Claudia wanted more. They passed a car that sat off the road but quickly jumped behind them as they flew by. Claudia's attention was pulled to the flashing lights in the rearview mirror.

"Someone behind us is flashing their lights," she said.

Samiyah turned around; the lights continued to flash. "Maybe it's one of the guys?"

"But why would they flash us and not just call."

"You're right," Samiyah said. "Keep driving."

The car sped up and was now on the girl's bumper. "They're blinding me," Claudia said.

Samiyah's phone rang. "She pulled it out of her handbag. "It's Jonas, maybe that's him behind us, I can't tell." She answered the phone peering through the back window. "Hey sweetheart is that you behind us?"

"I'm still in my father's home, but I'm leaving now."

"There's a car behind us flashing their lights. They're on our tail."

The car rear-ended them giving a little jab to the bumper. Samiyah and Claudia screamed.

"What's happening?" Jonas said alarmed.

"I don't know they just bumped us!"

The car swerved around coming to a hard stop in front of their vehicle cutting them off. The ladies screamed again as Claudia hit the brakes coming to a sharp stop.

"Where are you? Tell me where you are now!" Jonas commanded.

The passenger of the car got out. Samiyah watched as the guy walked to her side. With extreme force, he leaned back and struck the window with a crowbar busting the glass instantly.

"Aaaaaaaah! They screamed again. Shards of glass fell into Samiyah's lap as he reared back and struck the window over and over.

"Samiyah!" Jonas yelled. "Samiyah!"

There was shuffling through the phone. A second later a voice spoke. "Two for the price of one, it must be my lucky day."

"Who is this!"

"I would be offended by that question, but I have no time for it."

A foreboding ran throughout Jonas. "Kevin?" He questioned.

"See that's why I never get offended because I know before long you'll pick up on the sound of my voice."

"How's your night Jonas? I hope all is well considering."

"What are you doing?" he growled just about ready to break his phone in half.

"Getting your attention, I can't manage to get it otherwise, and it seems I'm not the only one. Man, you did a number on that pretty little assistant of yours. Broke her heart in pieces, I was going to take her, but she was all too forthcoming about giving up your father's location. You shouldn't put everything on your schedule, and you should know by now, not to trust women.

But since I've got your attention now, let me tell you what's going to happen next. This fight I have been so politely telling you about for the last couple of weeks is happening tonight. I need you to be there and not only do I need you to be there, I need you to win. See there's a lot of money at stake here, and as soon as you deliver, you will get your sweetheart back and her friend. Just to be clear, there are three fighters so bring you're A-game because you'll need to win against all three of them."

"I swear if you touch her." Jonas threatened.

"She won't be harmed unless... well, it's up to you. She is a beauty. I can see why she's caught your attention. I'm happy to have her in my company. We'll be in the old gymnasium off of Rucker's and Lance street, come through the back. "Oh, and don't even think about calling the police."

The call disconnected.

Jonas pushed passed his brothers, but they pulled back on him.

"Tell me what's going on?" Jaden said.

With a powerful shove, Jonas pushed Jaden against the car. "He has Samiyah!"

"Who has her?" They all questioned. Jonas let his brother go and opened the driver's side door jumping in.

"Jonas, tell me what is going on right now!" Martha demanded. He'd almost forgotten about her. Getting back out of the car Jonas reassured Martha.

"I'm going to get her back. I promise."

Martha's hands were in fists now. "Oh my God!" A look of terror was on her face.

"I'm sorry, I didn't think he would take it this far."

"I don't care about what you thought or who he is. This is all your fault!" Martha beat against his chest, but she might as well have been punching a brick wall for the damage it was doing. Jonas let Martha strike him, feeling all her emotions in his spirit. Martha cried and beat her fist into his chest before collapsing into him. He held her up.

"You're right, this is all my fault, but I promise you won't close your eyes to sleep tonight without her being there."

Christopher grabbed Martha, pulling her away from Jonas. Tears streamed down Martha's face as she thought of the horrible things that could be happening to her one and only baby girl. Jonas jumped back in the car. Jaden ran to the passenger side as Jonathon and Jordan climbed in the back while the other men jumped in a separate car. Jordan dialed Julian, Josiah, and Jacob while putting them on speaker phone. Jonas sped out of the driveway; his mind focused on getting to Samiyah.

"Who has Samiyah?" Jaden asked again getting down to the bottom of it.

"Kevin, he's been calling me for weeks wanting me to agree to an off the books fight and for weeks I've told him no. At first, I thought maybe he'd fell on hard times, but he's just greedy. He said there's a lot of money at stake, but he just made the biggest mistake of his life. Kevin has Claudia, too." Jonas glanced at Jaden. "I swear if something happens to her," Jonas said.

"Nothing's going to happen to either of them, we'll get them back."

As they got up the road, they came to a sudden stop as Claudia's car came into view sitting with the emergency lights blinking on the side of the road. Jonas' mind went wild with thoughts of what was happening to Samiyah. He sped off and drove to his home in Hyde Park pulled into the garage and switched vehicles. In the trunk of his Dodge Durango was a bag he kept with boxing gear inside.

Jordan stepped up to him. "I just made a phone call, I have a friend who's a detective—" Jonas cut him off.

"No, he said no police, I'm not risking it."

"He won't even know he's there," Jordan argued.

"Listen to me," Jonas said putting a hand on Jordan's shoulder with a firm grip. "I don't care what you do, but I have zero chances of messing this up. I'm going in there to get her first and then if your friend wants to show his face, fine, but not a minute sooner." Jordan had never seen Jonas so serious about any woman.

"Let me handle this," Jordan said. They jumped in the truck and drove to the gymnasium.

Chapter Twenty Eight

The entrance to the old gymnasium sat open and unattended as Jonas cruised through the gate. At first glance, it looked to be abandoned and empty, but Jonas knew better. Putting the truck in park, Jonas got out making his way to the trunk. He unzipped his black duffel bag with the large initials J. A. R. embedded on the flap. It had been a long time since he'd used this bag and the contents inside. Jonas grabbed what he needed and walked like a man on a mission towards the back door. It was also open and unattended.

Behind him, was Jaden and Jordan. The trio strolled with purpose down the long narrow hallway through an open door. A crowd of men stood in square formation posing as the outer layer of the makeshift ring. Most had placed their bets gambling on the winner of the fight while others were simply wanting a front row seat to see the undefeated boxer in all his glory once more. The crowd parted as Jonas entered. His eyes traveled from person to person but didn't find who he was looking for.

"Where's Kevin?" He asked his voice loud and menacing.

A rattle above his head caused him to look up at the green iron railing that outlined the wall above. Kevin placed his arms on the edge of the rail, his face barely seen in the dim light. Kevin's eyes shifted to Jaden and Jordan just as Jacob, Julian, and Josiah entered.

"You were supposed to come alone. Don't follow directions much?"

Jaden's face creased into a volatile menace as he bit down like a guard dog ready to attack. "You said no police. Where is she?"

Kevin reached back and slid his arm around Samiyah's waist pulling her close to his side; his hand tapping her slightly on her hip. "She's been by my side this whole time." A heinous smile curved up his lips. The movement turned him into a full fledge madman.

"I'll tell you what, let's make a deal. After I beat the crap out of whoever is stupid enough to enter this ring with me, I'll pay you, triple what you're making if you come down here and fight me yourself."

Kevin snickered, "Triple, huh?"

"Triple."

Kevin thought about the proposition. He wasn't a professional fighter but he was cocky enough to believe that once Jonas had gone through three men, he wouldn't have enough stamina left to withstand another fight if he made it through the three.

"Deal."

The curve of Jonas' lips told everyone that Jonas was looking forward to that part of the fight most. For a brief moment, he locked eyes with Samiyah. She didn't look afraid or sad. The look she shared with him was of love and adoration.

"Where's Claudia?"

Kevin glanced behind him and whistled. Seconds later Claudia appeared next to Samiyah, she looked more confused than anything. Jonas' focus went back to Samiyah, and she answered his unspoken question.

"We're fine."

Kevin clasped his hands together. "Yes, they're fine, now let's get this show on the road, shall we?"

A man walked into the ring and stood inches away from Jonas. His build was medium, but muscular and he stood three inches shorter than Jonas. The man tooted his rough lips in the air and blew kisses at Jonas in a mocking manner. Jonas put his teeth guard in and retrieved his gloves from Jaden.

"This is how this works. The only rule is no feet. This is not professional boxing, it's street boxing but using feet is a coward's way out. Stick with your hands. Whoever goes down first has to fight the next man until the last man is standing." Kevin paused, "And if for whatever reason you're still standing at the end of all three fights, Mr. Rose, then you'll have the pleasure of fighting yours truly."

Jonas was counting on it. A woman dressed in a scantily clad thin see through mini skirt, and bikini top walked into the ring holding a sign that read round 1. She circled the men completely and gave Jonas a wink before exiting. A bell sounded, and Jonas' competition started to dance in place, his body slightly bent with his boxing gloves blocking his face.

Mistake number one, *straighten your back,* Jonas heard Ned say in his mind as he watched the amateur fighter dance. With a tall solid stance, Jonas put his hands just above his chin, relaxing his arms, and shoulders with his elbows down. He wore the look of a wolf that had zoomed in on its prey. The man danced to the center of the ring and was attacked with three quick jabs to his midsection. There was a momentary shock, and the man dropped his hands for only a second but it was a second too long that left him exposed, and Jonas' uppercut forced him back with such intensity that his feet left the ground and he landed on his ass at the feet of the men crowding his area. They shouted for him to get up even going as far as to yank him off the ground and pushed him back into the ring.

Unfortunately for him, Jonas didn't give him a chance to recover, and Jonas attacked him again with a solid right then a firm left to his unprotected face. The man fell, his face red and crushed from the power of Jonas' blows. The men shouted and tried to make him get up again, but the man was laid out and already snoring. There would be no coming back from him.

Jonas looked towards Kevin and lifted one glove in the air. It was his promise that Jonas was most definitely coming for him. Kevin tried to play it off as if he was unbothered, but his uncomfortableness was written all over his face. He'd figured Jonas might beat the first guy, maybe even the second, but he didn't expect the man to go down so quickly.

For months, Kevin watched him train and box many times in live street fighting events, and he'd prevailed. Kevin was sure he had a winner but Jonas was too fast and his hits too robust. Although Kevin told Jonas he needed to win it was only to hype Jonas up. Kevin wasn't sure Jonas still had it in him, and he at least wanted Jonas to go a few rounds before getting knocked out. Kevin had placed his bet on the other guy, and already, he saw his money going down the drain.

The beaten man was dragged out of the ring, and the second man stepped in. He was the same height as Jonas with a muscular build that said he took occasional steroids with the veins that bulged in his arms. Standing on the rail, Samiyah shut her eyes briefly; she hated that Jonas had to deal with this. Samiyah knew how he felt about fighting and she was trying to hold it together. She needed to be strong for him and Claudia.

Besides, Samiyah didn't want to give Kevin the satisfaction of knowing she was worried. Not because she didn't think Jonas could win, but because of what he'd worked so hard for, going through counseling and coming out a better man in the long run. Whatever he would need from here on out, she would be there for him. It was no doubt in her mind about that. She watched the second boxer do the same dance that the first boxer had done that proved to be ineffective.

She looked to Jonas, his stance stayed strong, giving his punches power and range, his footing balanced and flexible. The other boxer threw punches but was met with Jonas' solid defense. After every punch the boxer threw his way, Jonas would step to the opposite side and throw a punch of his own that landed every time. It was infuriating his opponent, and Jonas knew it.

He was toying with the man, and Samiyah concluded that Jonas did it on purpose. The boxer tried to hold his ground and slip in a quick punch to Jonas' abdomen, but Jonas dropped his elbows blocking his punch and moved with agility teasing the man with three swift rock-hard punches to his face that took the man down to one knee.

"Ooooooh!" The crowd buzzed.

Jonas didn't give the would-be boxer a chance to get up. Instead, he finished him with a three-jab combination that forced the man to slouch and hit the ground. The noise from one side of the crowd indicated whose money had been put on the man and whose had been placed on Jonas. Some tried desperately to get the man up to no avail. Once again, Jonas set his sights on Kevin, lifting another hand that taunted him that soon it would be his turn. The third guy stepped in the ring, he stood face to face with Jonas built like a bull.

Samiyah tensed, the guy was huge in a mutant ninja turtle type of way. If she didn't know any better, she'd think someone had been experimenting on him in a secret lab, and he was made especially for a time such as this.

The fight began, and this time Jonas' opponent didn't dance. They roamed around in a slow circle sizing each other up. His opponent moved first with a quick jab to Jonas' abdomen which he in turn blocked. They continued to circle each other, and his opponent went in for a face jab that was blocked but swiftly landed a punch to Jonas' gut. Samiyah winced, Jonas didn't flinch. He calculated every move his opponent made. It was his usual tactic. The fighter seemed to have more speed and precision than his predecessors.

His opponent stepped in for another quick jab to his face, and Jonas bobbed sticking a quick jab to his opponent's throat making him buckle slightly. It was enough for Jonas to rain in three quick, vicious jabs to his face and when his opponent tried to block, Jonas laid another duo of brutal jabs to his chest. Jonas' hands worked in sync as he jabbed, blocked, crouched and jabbed again.

Samiyah felt Kevin flinch beside her, but her eyes stayed glued to the fight. Kevin reached over and grabbed Samiyah's arm pulling her into his light. He planted a kiss on her face and padded her butt. The movement was not missed by Jonas, and he temporarily lost his focus with a glance towards them.

Samiyah jerked back and smacked Kevin across the face and Jonas was hit with a combination that took him to his knees.

"Noooo!" Samiyah screamed, and her heart sank.

Jonas recovered quickly punching his opponent in his precious jewels. If Kevin wanted to play dirty, so would he. His opponent buckled immediately giving Jonas the advantage to take him down. His combination rained down on the man in succession blow after gut wrenching blow. He fell to the side, and the crowd was going crazy.

Jonas stood and spit. Jordan and Jaden stepped in to supply Jonas with water. Sweat glistened Jonas forehead, and blood sat where his lip had been cut open.

Kevin slipped brass knuckles on his hands and left the railing with Samiyah and Claudia in tow. His arrogance was thick, and he stepped into the ring.

"As promised," Kevin said gesturing toward Samiyah.

"Baby, let's just go please," she begged.

"By the way," Kevin countered, "she tastes delicious." He licked his lips.

Jonas removed his gloves and tossed them to the side. In an instant, Jonas was on top of Kevin throwing punches faster than he ever had before. His adrenaline was on an all-time high as he pummeled Kevin's face. Blood seeped through Kevin nose, mouth and ears as Jonas hit him with the strength of an iron fist. Hands pulled at Jonas as his brothers struggled to pull him off the bloody, battered man. Rage was all Jonas felt and not even his brothers could snap him out of it.

"Jonas please you're going to kill him!" Samiyah screamed.

Her voice seemed to do it. Jonas punched him again for good measure and rose like a raging bull. He turned to Samiyah, and she withdrew. Jonas took a step toward her, and she took another step back. It dawned on him what he must have looked like. His face softened, and his fist unclenched.

"Baby," he said, "You know I would never hurt you."

Tears dropped down Samiyah's cheeks, "Of course I know that. I didn't mean too..." she sighed, "I've never seen you this way."

The crowd dispersed as police officers swarmed the room.

"Let's go!"

His brothers said. They moved in sync and made their way to the car. Jaden jumped in the driver's seat, Claudia the passenger and Jonas and Samiyah in the back. Jordan jumped in with his other brothers that were waiting for the group at the entrance. They hightailed it out of there and regrouped back at his penthouse where their father and Samiyah's mother waited.

Chapter Twenty Nine

"Let me look at you." Samiyah surveyed Jonas' face. The last opponent was the only one who'd gotten a hand on him. His lip was cut, but it was minor. His hands, however, displayed multiple cuts with a slight swell. Samiyah was dismayed. "You could've broken your hand. What were you thinking?" She grabbed the hot cloth that was soaking in steamy water and squeezed it, applying it tenderly to his knuckles.

"I was thinking about you." Her eyes met his, "I'm sorry. The last thing I want to do is lose control. Even though that's the case, I've never felt a need for someone the way I feel for you. It goes without saying that I never want to see you hurt or in harm's way. Since the moment I met you, I've felt a responsibility towards your well-being. At first, I couldn't figure it out, and I continued to tell myself to dismiss it but now..."

Samiyah continued to pad his hands.

"Now what?" she asked.

"Now I know that I'm in love with you, Samiyah Manhattan. Irrevocably, in love. With everything that you are and everything that you do. Your respect for others, your motivation, your selflessness." His fingers enfolded hers. "Marry me."

Samiyah froze, her heart beat a million times a minute. He couldn't be serious. He must be crazy, she thought.

"Don't run," he kissed her hands. "Don't look to reason," he kissed her lips, "Just marry me."

"Jonas, please." Samiyah searched his eyes. Jonas didn't understand the magnitude of his question, Samiyah thought.

"I know what I'm asking you and you must know by now that I'm not the playboy you think I am. You're the love of my life. I'll beg if you want me to. He slid off the couch to his knees. "Samiyah Manhattan please do me this honor and spend the rest of your life with me."

She was crying now. How could she not? "Oh my God." She slid her arms around his neck and cried soft tears.

"Is that a yes?"

Claudia entered the room. "Girl if you don't answer that man!"

Jonas smiled, and his brothers followed suit.

"Yes, of course!" Samiyah cried.

Whistles, handclaps, whoops and shouts flooded the room.

"Congratulations brother!" Jaden said. He slapped Jonas on the back, but Jonas was too focused on his bride to be. With tears still in her eyes, they kissed and held each other tight. Finally, Jonas stood lifting Samiyah with him.

"I love you," he said.

"I love you, too."

As Claudia watched on, she squealed and did a little jig. "Ooooohh you lucky, lucky, girl!"

After all the commotion died down, Samiyah approached her mom. "Are you okay?"

Martha Jean observed her child. "I'm the one who should be asking you."

Samiyah held her hands out. "I'm fine. He never touched me, well not in the way you may have thought."

Martha looked alarmed.

"He tried to feel me up as a distraction technique. It's bizarre, Jonas told me Kevin wanted him to fight and win, but during the match, Kevin attempted to distract Jonas. I don't think Kevin thought Jonas would win and he was bluffing about wanting him to all along."

Martha shrugged. "I'm just glad you're okay." A tear fell from Martha's eye and Samiyah's arms wrapped around her.

"Don't cry mom, please, everything is fine."

"I could've lost you. All this time, I've been, so hell bent on you staying clear of men and in an instant, you could've been gone." She sighed. "That man really loves you. I've honestly never seen anything like it."

Samiyah smiled, slowly rubbing her mom's back as their embrace tightened. "I'm so glad you can see that."

"I'd be crazy not to admit it. You may have truly done it this time."

Samiyah pulled back astonished. "Are you saying you think he's the one?"

Martha smirked. "I ain't saying all of that." They laughed. "But I do approve. He's good for you." Now tears were falling from Samiyah's eyes. "Awe, don't cry baby girl." Martha wiped them away.

"That's all I've ever wanted."

"I'm sorry I've been so hard on you. You're grown, this is your life, and I should trust you to make the best decisions for it."

Samiyah placed a kiss on her forehead. "Who are you and what have you done with my mother?"

"Oh, stop it."

"If you want to stay the night mom, it's A-Okay. There's plenty of room."

"I don't want to be a bother."

"You won't be. I promise; besides, you've got a wedding to help me plan."

"When one door closes," Martha chimed.

"Another one opens," Samiyah finished.

They hugged each other and Samiyah led her to the guest room.

The following day, Jonas stepped into his office. "Sandra, cancel my meetings for today."

"Sir?"

He turned to her. "You heard me correctly, cancel my meetings and see me in my office in fifteen minutes."

"Yes sir."

Sandra grabbed the receiver and went about canceling Jonas' appointments. She had never seen him so serious before and in the office in casual wear. Amanda strolled past her and tapped lightly on the door frame. Jonas looked up. "Come in Amanda and close the door please."

Amanda swallowed the lump in her throat and glided into the room shutting the door behind her.

"Have a seat."

Amanda sat down in one of the comfortable leather chairs, and Jonas sat in the one adjacent to her leaning forward so she could look nowhere but his face.

"I want to start off by saying, I apologize."

Amanda seemed genuinely astonished.

"You came to me as a friend and asked if I would place a bid on you at the auction and I didn't come through. I never meant to hurt you, and I had every intention of placing a bid. You see, I'm in love with Samiyah Manhattan, and I'm going to marry her. I didn't know that she would be a part of the auction. If I did, I would've made sure one of my brothers placed the highest bid for you. That way you still would've been in good hands."

He sat back and rubbed his jaw. "Throughout the time you've been my assistant, things have run rather smoothly, and there's never been a breach of contract. However, I need to ask you, do you feel like I've behaved unprofessionally towards you, at any point and time?"

Amanda hesitated.

"You can speak freely," he said.

She sighed, "No, you've been nothing but professional. I mean you're very charming, so it's easy to be..." she reached back and massaged her neck, "taken by you."

"I understand."

Amanda bit down on her lip. "I love you Jonas, and I don't quite understand why you would pick someone else to love over me. I've been here for you and done things no assistant should have to do so excuse me if I don't get it."

"What have you done that you feel no assistant should have to do?"

"For one, send flowers and a 'thank you we had a nice time but it's over cards' to women you've dated. It's embarrassing."

"I'm sorry you feel that way. For the longest time, I saw you as irreplaceable. You have no idea how many assistants I went through before hiring you. But honestly, the current events reveal that's no longer the case."

"I didn't mean to fall in love with you, I just did."

Jonas nodded his head up and down. "You also put my fiancé in an unbearable position. She could've been killed."

Amanda gasped covering her mouth.

"Is that what you wanted?"

"Of course not, I was so angry, I just..." her eyes watered.

"You're fired." He stood. "Turn in your set of keys, please."

"Jonas..." Amanda stuttered, "Mr. Rose, I promise it'll never happen again."

He peered at her. "You seem surprised. Did you think I would keep you on board after what you've done?"

Her eyes shifted away then back to him. She stood up. "I thought you would forgive me! I thought you would understand."

"I do forgive you. However, you gave out my personal information. That never should've happened, under any circumstances."

Her small frame shook. "Please!" Amanda begged.

"You'll have a hefty severance package. Unfortunately, I can't write you a letter of recommendation, and I wouldn't put me on the call list for a reference either."

Tears streamed down Amanda's face. There was a knock at the door. "Come in."

Sandra floated quietly into the room. "Sir."

"Yes Sandra, I'll need another assistant as soon as possible. Go through the list we have on file please and set up some interviews."

Sandra glanced from Amanda's wilted frame back to Jonas. "Anything else, sir?"

"Yes, I'll need you to step in until I've replaced Amanda."

Amanda clutched her purse and walked stunned towards the exit. After she left, Jonas closed the door.

"Have a seat Sandra."

Sandra hoped this conversation wouldn't end like the one between him and Amanda.

Jonas perched his hip on the desk in front of her. "It has come to my attention that Amanda had romantic feelings for me. I don't reciprocate those feelings. She breached her contract, and I had to let her go. Now, I know you know, she's been with me for years but make no mistake, I will not tolerate insubordination. I'm newly engaged." Sandra's eyes widened. "Does that present a problem for you?"

"No sir."

"I need you professional at all times, can you do that for me?"

"Yes, of course."

"No more flirting or lingering in my doorway."

Sandra's face lit up beet red. "Um, no, of course not."

"Good, now that that's out of the way. Make sure to have a list of interviews set up by the weekend."

"Shall I change the passcodes that Amanda has?"

"I'm doing that myself; I've already started."

"Okay, will there be anything else?" Sandra was all too eager to flee the office.

"No, that will be all."

Before Jonas could count to ten, Sandra was gone.

Epilogue

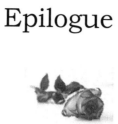

The grains of sand sank between Samiyah's toes as her feet landed on rose petals. With tentative steps, Samiyah glided between row on row of white chairs filled with family, friends, and associates. In their eyesight, she was radiant and gracious. They'd come back to where it all began, San Juan, Puerto Rico. Samiyah suggested they honor Jonas' mother by saying their vows where his parents had said theirs. It made Jonas' heart swell, and his eyes fill with a mist of tears.

Darkness covered the sky, and the moon sat bright in the heavens. It was a perfect scenery with stars sprinting across the atmosphere. The beach was decorated with night lights that wrapped around chairs, bouquets of flowers, and the golden arch standing over her groom.

In Jonas' eyes, Samiyah was a goddess, the most beautiful person he'd ever seen. Covered in a red and white wedding gown that hugged her curves down to her knees. It was her desire to walk barefooted, and Jonas didn't mind at all. Samiyah's hair flowed down her back with red jewels drawing a line down the middle. Jonas' wedding day was always a blur in his eyes.

He didn't see it coming, his mom was his whole heart, and he couldn't imagine loving someone the way his father had loved her, then losing them to such violence. It had rendered him incapable of opening his heart. At least that's what he thought.

Samiyah came into his life and broke through a barrier he thought was unbreakable and she was the best thing that ever happened to him. When she stepped in front of him, Jonas wanted to remove her veil instantly but held back for the sake of tradition. The pastor started with dearly beloved and Jonas didn't hear anything else. His heart beat fast in his chest, and he could swear it would explode at any moment.

A grin spread across his clean-shaven face. The excitement was like a ball of energy. As the pastor spoke, Jonas pulled Samiyah's hand to his lips and kissed the back. Her eyes sparkled, and a few tears landed on her russet cheeks. Jonas would give Samiyah all she longed for and more.

Samiyah was on pins and needles. The last six months had been a whirlwind of preparation and things had come together in a fantasy fairytale. In her opinion, the time frame was still too short to plan the wedding, but it couldn't have come fast enough for Jonas. She loved that he loved her so assiduously. It was contagious, and her love for him drenched her completely. Jonas broad shoulders filled his Armani suit in polished, exquisite fashion. Thick black lashes hovered over his possessive stare sending a shrill of excitement crawling down Samiyah's spine. His mouth moved slow and sexy.

"I do," he said.

She barely heard it. Everything was now moving in slow motion. It was happening, her second chance. She didn't beg for it, didn't even want it, and yet it had found her faster than she could blink. Samiyah held no regrets. Her mother was in attendance. Martha had given them her blessings, helped Samiyah plan the wedding, and picked out a dress.

Samiyah gained a father, six brothers, and three sisters who were all in attendance. Samiyah even referred to Norma as Auntie Norm. It was overwhelming; more than anything she could ask for. But most importantly, Samiyah gained the man of her dreams; the love of her existence and without a doubt, she loved him more than life itself. It bewildered Samiyah. She didn't think a love like this was possible.

Suddenly, Samiyah noticed the silence. Jonas continued to level her with a watchful gaze. Quickly Samiyah glanced around; they were waiting on her. A radiant smile floated across her face.

"I do."

"With the power vested in me—" before the pastor could finish, her veil was lifted, and Jonas drew her in for a succulent kiss. Thunderous applause rose from the crowd. The tears had a mind of their own now, streaming fast down both of their faces. Chocolate mint and sweet honey lay fresh on their palates as they continued the stimulating kiss they couldn't seem to pull apart from.

"I now pronounce you Mr. and Mrs. Jonas Alexander Rose."

More thunderous applause. Jonas finally released her lips, long enough to breathe and kiss her again.

"I love you," his dark voice groveled.

"I love you, too," Samiyah crooned.

They turned to the crowd and waved, Samiyah blowing kisses to her mom and best friend, Claudia. When Samiyah looked back to Jonas, his eyes were on her. He winked, and they ran down the aisle into the night.

The End

Enjoying Falling for a Rose Series? Grab the next installment which follows Jaden Alexander Rose and Claudia Stevens as they venture into a thing called love in, Enough.

Hey reading family, thanks for rocking with me on this roller-coaster ride! I hope you enjoyed this book as much as I enjoyed writing it. If so, take a moment and leave a review on Amazon. Check the next page for other books I have in store and be sure to sign up for my newsletter!

XOXO - Stephanie

Safe with Me

More Books by Stephanie Nicole Norris

Contemporary Romance
- Everything I Always Wanted (A Friends to Lovers Romance)
- Safe With Me (Falling for a Rose Book One)
- Enough (Falling for a Rose Book Two)
- Only If You Dare (Falling For a Rose Book Three)

Romantic Suspense Thrillers
- Beautiful Assassin
- Beautiful Assassin 2 Revelations
- Mistaken Identity
- Trouble In Paradise
- Vengeful Intentions (Trouble In Paradise 2)
- For Better and Worse (Trouble In Paradise 3)
- Until My Last Breath (Trouble In Paradise 4)

Christian Romantic Suspense

- Broken
- Reckless Reloaded

Crime Fiction
- Prowl
- Prowl 2
- Hidden (Coming Soon)

Fantasy

- Golden (Rapunzel's F'd Up Fairytale)

Non-Fiction

- Against All Odds (Surviving the Neonatal Intensive Care Unit) *Non-Fiction

About the Author

Stephanie Nicole Norris is an author from Chattanooga Tennessee with a humble beginning. She was raised with six siblings by her mother Jessica Ward. Always being a lover of reading, during Stephanie's teenage years her joy was running to the bookmobile to read stories by R. L. Stine.

After becoming a young adult, her love for romance sparked leaving her captivated by heroes and heroines alike. With a big imagination and a creative heart, Stephanie penned her first novel Trouble In Paradise and self-published it in 2012. Her debut novel turned into a four book series full of romance, drama, and suspense. As a prolific writer, Stephanie's catalog continues to grow. Her books can be found on Amazon dot com. Stephanie is inspired by the likes of Donna Hill, Eric Jerome Dickey, Jackie Collins, and more. She currently resides in Tennessee with her husband and two-year-old son.

https://stephanienicolenorris.com/

Made in the USA
Coppell, TX
03 November 2021